UnleashHer

Real Stories of Healing
from the Inside Out

An Anthology Created for Women by Women

Copyright Page for UnleashHer: Real Stories of Healing from the Inside Out

Publisher: RC Academy
Editing & Compilation: Roberta Campbell and Chantelle Sprenger
Cover Design: Jade Olszewski
Interior Layout & Formatting: Roberta Campbell, Chantelle Sprenger and Paige Knechtly
First Edition: December 2025
ISBN: 979-8-9939843-0-8

Table of Contents

Disclaimer 4

Dedication 5

Acknowledgements 6

Endorsements 7

Foreword...11

Introduction 14

Chapter 1. The Fall and Rise of Roberta Campbell 17

Chapter 2. Success is a Sure Thing for You 23

Chapter 3. The Girl in the Mirror 33

Chapter 4. Visual Frequency Medicine: Born
            In the Fire 43

Chapter 5. The Long Road Home....................................53

Chapter 6. My Testimony My Victory 63

Chapter 7. When the Body Screams What the
            Heart Can't Say 73

Chapter 8. Choosing Life...83

Chapter 9. The Greatest Gift...93

Chapter 10. Make It Till You Make It 103

Chapter 11. Is the Glass Half Empty or Half Full? 113

Conclusion 123

About the Authors 124

References..130

Disclaimer

This book contains personal stories of growth, healing, and transformation. The experiences shared by each author are their own and are offered to inspire, educate, and inform.

The content in this anthology is not intended to replace professional, medical, psychological, or spiritual advice. If you are experiencing physical or mental health challenges, please seek support from a qualified healthcare provider, counselor, or licensed therapist.

Some stories may contain sensitive topics such as trauma, grief, abuse, or loss, which could be triggering for some readers. Please proceed with care and compassion for your own wellbeing.

While the authors and publisher have made every effort to ensure the accuracy of the information contained within this book, we make no guarantees about the results you may achieve from applying the concepts, practices, or insights discussed. Your journey is unique, and results will vary for each individual.

The publisher, editor, and contributors assume no responsibility or liability for any actions taken by readers as a result of reading this book.

Please engage with the material with self-awareness and discernment.

Dedication

This book is dedicated to every woman who has ever felt silenced, unseen, or unworthy. May you find your voice, reclaim your power, and rise with courage. To the brave souls who shared their stories within these pages:

Your vulnerability is a gift.
Your healing lights the path for others.
Your words will echo in the hearts of women around the world, reminding them that they, too, are not alone.

To our daughters, sisters, mothers, and friends both past, present, and future: may this collection be a reminder that your story matters, your dreams are valid, and it is never too late to rewrite your next chapter.

To the younger versions of ourselves, the little girls who once dreamed big dreams:

We see you.
We honor you.
We are living for you now.

And to the incredible authors who poured their hearts into these chapters: thank you for your courage, your honesty, and your willingness to step into the light. By sharing your stories, you've created a ripple effect of healing, hope, and transformation that will reach farther than you'll ever know.

This book exists because you dared to say yes to your truth.
With gratitude, love, and unwavering hope,
this is for you.

Acknowledgements

With deep gratitude, I want to thank the incredible women who contributed their stories for *UnleashHer*. Your courage to speak your truth and share your healing has created a powerful ripple of inspiration that will touch lives around the world.

To every woman reading this, know that your story matters. Healing is not a destination; it's a journey of remembering who you are. May these pages remind you that your power has always been within you.

To my family, friends, mentors, and coaches: thank you for your unwavering love, support, and guidance. Each of you has played a role in helping me become the woman I am today.

And to God, thank you for your presence in every step of this journey, for turning pain into purpose, and for showing me that we are never truly alone.

Together, we are *UnleashHer:* rising in love, truth, and authenticity.

With love and gratitude,

Roberta Campbell

Creator of *UnleashHer*

Endorsements

UnleashHer is a powerful reminder that healing begins when we allow our inner light to be seen. As I read these stories, I felt the essence of what I teach- that wholeness truly is the new power, and that when there is no enemy within, the outside world loses its power to wound us. Each woman's journey reflects the very principles I hold dear: stillness that reveals truth, healing that reconnects us to ourselves, and the courage to rise into the fullest expression of who we are.
This anthology beautifully mirrors the work I do in guiding leaders through self-awareness, self-care, and ultimately self-actualization. These stories bridge past and future, awaken possibility, and remind us that our resilience is shared. I saw pieces of my own journey in these pages, and I believe every reader will discover a spark of their own light here too.

LORETTA MONARENG, CEO & FOUNDER, THE MONARENG GROUP, LLC

Ashley has an incredible amount of life experience and wisdom to share. Her resilience is second to none...her real-life stories and how far she has come is remarkable! Her passion for life, for wellness, for healing is more than admirable!! It is purely inspirational! You can feel the power pouring out of her words. Highly recommend this read!

ANGELLE PRIMEAU
INTUITIVE GUIDE AND MENTOR

My Testimony, My Victory is a powerful testament to the courage it takes to turn inner silence into a voice of strength. In this heartfelt chapter, the author invites us into her journey of discovering that the most significant burdens often carry the seeds of our deepest empowerment. Margaret shows us how facing those hidden wounds and embracing the lessons within them can transform not only our own lives but also those of those we guide. This chapter is a beautifully honest celebration of turning personal trials into a purposeful victory.

"It's an inspiring read for anyone ready to find strength in their own story."

ROBINA ABRAMSON-WALLING.
BSN,MN,PHD(C)DNM(C)

What a truly amazing collection of heartfelt stories filled with courage, inspiration, and strength. This book will make you laugh and cry. Thanks to these female writers for sharing their incredible journeys.

JENNIFER MICHAELSON

What a powerful testament to the resilience and unstoppable spirit of women. Each chapter is a reminder of courage. This book is not only inspiring but it shows the extraordinary impact of ordinary women who chose to stand tall in the face of challenge. A must read for anyone seeking hope.

Jody Sebastian

There are details in the book that were particularly impactful and a game changer for me personally is in Chapter Ten, *Make it Till you Make It*, by Sabrina. She states "The God of yesterday is still the God of today." Conveys to me that signifies God's unchanging character nature. Being constant and reliable through faithfulness and love. The God that can remain trusted and relied upon just as powerful today as in the past.

UnleashHer is more than just a book; it's a roadmap to healing involving a journey of self-reflection, acceptance and active coping. The book addresses each individual story that involves multiple stages and steps to heal from hurt and trauma. I have no doubt that this book will become an indispensable resource for anyone seeking self-awareness. I wholeheartedly endorse this book and believe many readers will benefit from reading it.

Aaron Morley

Reading this book has made me feel seen, heard, understood and most importantly validated. It is an amazing feeling to know that you are not alone. As a woman, I feel that I am expected to do it all, know it all, handle it all- and remain calm while doing it. It has felt in the past that I could not share or express how I was feeling or what I was experiencing for fear of being misunderstood, dismissed or excluded.

After reading this powerful book, I now feel empowered to share my thoughts, feelings and experiences with others. This book has given me the courage to share my own truth and not to be worried about judgement. While reading the chapters of this book, I cried, I empathized, I prayed and I related to so much.

I am so blessed and thankful that God has put this book, and Margaret Tapogna Gatzonis, into my hands. I hope that this book is placed in many women's hands so that they too can see the light that it brings. I encourage anyone who has felt alone, scared, anxious, worried or confused to read this book and connect to the contributors.

These women are here to help. They will outstretch their hands and heal you from the inside out. Your heart, your mind and your body will thank you.

Alison Brotschol
Mom, Pre-K Teacher & Coordinator for The Franklin Square District

When asked to critique *UnleashHer* I was excited due to the fact that I had just published and won International Impact Book Awards for my books which dealt with relationships, Self-Help and Personal Development where the focus was on Female Goddesses and Men dealing with their mate once she entered menopause. My books, although not intended for women, those who read it found it inspiring.

After reading *UnleashHer* I do believe that every MAN needs to read this book, so that they can experience the deep, inner feelings, turmoil, trials and tribulations women go through, that we as men have no clue of, or because of their suffering in silence, as many of the contributors of the book spoke of, we haven't noticed or take the time to notice.

Respectfully Submitted,
James Kelly Jr., M.S. Ed.: CEO/CFO S.E.M.A.J. Productions/Publishing Inc.

Roberta Campbell and contributing authors you have put vision to paper, you laid it all out there with conviction, passion, love, and authenticity. You created a blueprint for whoever reads your stories, they will learn they can get through anything with a willing spirit. Writers were uncensored, genuine, resulting in a powerful blessing to occur suddenly in your reader's life. You became the message so you could convey it to someone who will be grateful for your words of lessons, wisdom, and experiences.
Failure and rise is always the beginning of something new; first you fail to anticipate so you can move forward. Faith is the anchor that energized and encouraged you the authors to collaborate and share these remarkable stories in depth! This book is one to read and take the challenges to move forward as these writers did!

Elder Theresa Hart and bestselling author of "The Enemy in the Inner Me"

Foreword

UnleashHer: Real Stories of Healing from the Inside Out
by Roberta Campbell and Contributing Authors

A Foreword by Kathleen Cameron
Bestselling Author | Queen of Manifestation | CEO, Diamond Academy

From the moment I met Roberta Campbell, I felt her light. She is the kind of woman who walks into a room and immediately makes you feel seen, safe, and inspired. Her energy is radiant, her presence is warm, and her mission is unmistakable: to help women remember who they are. Roberta is not just a teacher of transformation; she is a living, breathing example of it.
I had the honor of mentoring Roberta in one of my Diamond Academy programs, where I watched her evolve in the most powerful ways. She showed up with a hunger for truth, a deep desire to heal, and a vision far bigger than her circumstances. And she didn't just dream of becoming a woman of impact; she became her. Over the years, I've watched Roberta step into her calling with grace, courage, and spiritual authority, and now she's created something that will change lives.

UnleashHer is a profound and necessary book. Within these pages, Roberta and a community of brave women share their stories not from a place of pain, but from a place of power. They don't just tell you what they've been through, they show you what's possible when you choose to heal, rise, and take full ownership of your life. These are not just stories. These are activations. Each one is a mirror reflecting the truth that your past does not define you; your decision to become does.

As the CEO of Diamond Academy, a two-time bestselling author, and a spiritual leader who has mentored thousands of individuals worldwide in the art of manifestation and identity transformation, I have seen firsthand what it takes to overcome limitations and rewrite your story. I've walked this path myself from self-doubt to self-mastery, and I've had the privilege of guiding countless others to do the same. I know transformation when I see it. And what Roberta and these women have created is nothing short of extraordinary.

UnleashHer will move you. It will stir something inside of you that's been dormant. It will awaken your heart to what's possible when you choose to do the deep work from the inside out. Whether you're in the middle of your own healing or just beginning to hear the whisper that there's more for you, this book is a guidepost on the path home to yourself. These stories are proof that the journey may be messy, but it is holy, and you don't have to walk it alone.

To Roberta and every contributing author: thank you for your courage. You have turned your pain into purpose, and your stories will ripple through generations.
To the reader: take your time with this book. Let it move through you. Let it remind you that you, too, are meant to rise.

With immense pride and love,
Kathleen Cameron
CEO, Diamond Academy
Bestselling Author & Queen of Manifestation

"Healing begins when we share our stories, open our hearts, and allow ourselves to be seen."
RC

Introduction

Welcome to *UnleashHer*, a collection of stories from extraordinary women who chose to rise, heal, and embrace their true selves.

This anthology was created with one powerful intention: to remind you that you are not alone. Every woman carries a story: of struggle, triumph, heartbreak, and resilience. For too long, many of us have kept those stories buried deep within, afraid of judgment, rejection, or simply believing our voices didn't matter. But here, in these pages, you'll find women who chose to break free.

Each chapter is a window into a soul. The women who wrote them have been through challenges they never imagined they could survive: trauma, loss, grief, heartbreak, identity struggles, illness, reinvention, and transformation. Through it all, they discovered something profound: within every ending is the seed of a new beginning.

When I first dreamed of *UnleashHer*, I knew it had to be more than just a book. I envisioned a movement. A community of women who lift one another higher, who refuse to play small, who embrace authenticity, and who dare to create lives filled with meaning, love, and joy.

This anthology is a testament to what happens when women come together to heal, to share, and to rise.
As you turn these pages, you will laugh, cry, and most importantly, you will see yourself.

You may find pieces of your own story in these words. You may be inspired to forgive, to release, to dream again, and to step boldly into the woman you were always meant to be. This book is not just about the stories you'll read, it's about the story you are living right now.

As you journey through each chapter, I invite you to do so with an open heart. Allow yourself to be moved, challenged, and inspired. Some stories may feel familiar, others may open your eyes to new perspectives. Either way, I believe these pages found their way to you for a reason.

Because here's the truth:
Your story matters.
Your voice matters.
You matter.

This is your invitation to rise, to heal, and to reclaim your power. To every author who said yes to this project: thank you for your courage, your honesty, and your willingness to bare your soul so others could see the light in their own darkness.

And to you, the reader: may these stories ignite something deep within you like a spark of hope, a whisper of possibility, a reminder that you, too, are limitless.

Welcome to *UnleashHer*.
Welcome home.

With love and gratitude,

Roberta Campbell

Chapter 1

The Fall and Rise of Roberta Campbell

After the Storm

There comes a moment in every woman's life when she looks around and realizes, something must change. For me, that moment came after hitting rock bottom. I remember sitting alone, surrounded by a life that no longer felt like my own. I had tried to hold everything together for so long-my family, my business, my image-but inside, I was falling apart.

When I look back now, I see that this was the exact moment when my new life began.
Because before you can rise, you must first face the fall.

When I made the decision to change my life, it wasn't easy.
In fact, it was terrifying. I didn't have the money.
I didn't have confidence. But I had a burning desire and a knowing deep within me that I was meant for more. I joined Bob Proctor's year-long coaching program even though it meant putting the balance on a credit card. I was so full of fear that night, I didn't sleep.
But my intuition told me this was my chance to rewrite my story.

That one decision shifted everything. For the first time, I took full responsibility for my life-where I was, how I got there, and who I was becoming. And that ownership became my foundation for growth.

I immersed myself in personal development and energy work. I started to see my patterns, self-limiting beliefs and programming that had shaped me since childhood. I realized I'd been living from a place of lack, fear, and control. I was chasing security because, deep down, I never felt safe.

Old Wounds and Awakening

As the youngest of four, I spent a lot of time alone. My brother died before I was born, and although I never met him, his absence was like a quiet ache in our home. I remember feeling confused seeing photos of my brother, and wondering what happened to him. I remember asking my mom what happened, but the pain of losing a child was too difficult to discuss.
We didn't heal. We just kept going.

Growing up, affection wasn't something we expressed easily. So, I learned to hold my emotions in, to stay strong, to keep smiling no matter what.

However, that strength came with an emotional cost. It made it hard for me to love deeply. To trust. To receive. I became a perfectionist and a control freak-trying to fix everything around me because I didn't know how to feel safe within myself.

It took years and two incredible coaches to help me see it. I invested thousands of dollars, spent countless nights journaling, crying, and forgiving myself and others. With each layer I released, I began to see myself more clearly.

I began to understand that those moments of pain weren't punishments-they were lessons. Each one was teaching me how to surrender, how to heal, and how to return to the woman I was always meant to be.
After my year with Bob Proctor, I joined Kathleen Cameron's community-a group of powerful women rising in consciousness. It was there that I began to understand my worth, to truly feel what it meant to live as my higher self. My energy shifted, and for the first time in a long time, I felt unstoppable.
And then…life tested me again.

After publishing my first book, *She Looks Fine,* my daughter was in another accident. The fear, the grief, the exhaustion-I felt it all wash over me again. I remember thinking, "How could this be happening again?"

But this time, something was different.
I knew this wasn't the end. It was an invitation to deepen my faith. I had to lose everything I thought I needed to realize how truly blessed I already am.

In those moments of stillness, when I had nothing left to hold onto, I found something stronger...faith. Not the kind of faith that wishes or hopes, but the kind that knows. The kind that holds you when everything around you is falling apart.

Healing in Stillness

When I moved to the country, everything slowed down. I found peace in the quiet. I now enjoyed the sound of the wind, the sunrise, the space between my thoughts. In that stillness, I found God again.

I asked for healing, and I allowed it to come. I cried every day for weeks...not the kind of cry that leaves you empty, but the kind that frees your soul.
I let go of old pain and old stories that no longer served me.

And in that release, I found clarity. I remembered who I was. I remembered that little girl who used to dream of being a teacher, an actress, a singer, a storyteller, a giver of hope. She had always been there-waiting for me to come home to her.

From that place of peace, I began to rebuild. Slowly, gently, one decision at a time.

Becoming Her

The healing didn't happen overnight. It took time. It took grace. It took a willingness to believe in myself again, even when I didn't know how things would work out.

But I stayed committed to becoming the woman I knew I could be...
strong,
confident,
authentic,
loving, and free.
I began to act as her-my higher self-long before I felt ready.

Then something magical happened. Opportunities began to appear. I was guided to create again. I poured my heart into my interactive journal, *Unleashed: The Seven-Minute Gratitude and Manifestation Journal.* That project became my bridge between who I was and who I was becoming.

It reignited my passion and gave me the confidence to take a quantum leap of faith.

Once I published *Unleashed*, women began reaching out and asking for guidance, wanting to share their stories, craving the same kind of healing and transformation I had found. I realized this was no longer about me. This was about us. So, I listened to that inner nudge, that divine whisper that said, "It's time."

That's how this anthology was born. *UnleashHer: Real Stories of Healing from the Inside Out* is not just a collection of stories-it's a movement. A safe space for women to rise, to be their true self, to be seen, to heal, and to inspire others to do the same.

My powerful energy attracted these incredible women into my life-women who, like me, have faced unimaginable challenges and found their way back to light, faith, and freedom.

Your Time to Rise

If you're reading this, I want you to know something…
You are not broken. You are not behind. You are exactly where you are meant to be.

The fact that you are here means your soul is ready. You are ready to rise and to step into your power, to heal from the inside out, and to live a life that feels good on every level.

I know because I've been there. I know what it's like to lose everything, to question your worth, to wonder if things will ever get better. I also know the power of choosing yourself and of saying yes even when it's scary.

So, if you're standing at the edge of a decision right now, listen to that still, calm, small voice inside you. The one that whispers, "You were made for more."

This is your sign.
This is your moment.
It's your time to **RISE.**

And when you're ready, reach out, because I'm here to help.

Roberta Campbell

Chapter 2
Success is a Sure Thing for You

The Fortune That Found Me

The night of my grade 12 graduation, the room buzzed with certainty, university plans, scholarships and futures unfolding. Everyone seemed to know where they were headed. I didn't. All I had was a heart full of questions, a stomach full of nerves, and a small yellow slip of paper that would change everything.

The details of that night have faded, but one moment is still crystal clear. I'll never forget opening a fortune cookie and seeing seven bold black words that changed everything:

"Success is a sure thing for you."

I froze. It felt like the universe had whispered into my ear. Something shifted— those words wrapped around my heart like a warm hand, quietly assuring me that I'd be okay.

At seventeen, I wasn't spiritual or searching for signs. However, those words found me anyway. They became an anchor I didn't know I needed, a flicker of hope for a life that could look different from my past. I couldn't explain it. I just knew they meant something.

I carried that fortune in my wallet for years, pulling it out when life got hard, and it did, often. That line became my declaration, my quiet belief. Long before I knew the power of thought or energy, I was already practicing it. That fortune wasn't just a piece of paper. It was a promise. The truth is, nothing in my life suggested success should've been mine.
But somehow, I believed it anyway.

The Storm Before the Light

My childhood felt like a battlefield. The air at home was thick with tension that could turn without warning. Words became weapons, and the walls held their breath, waiting for the storm to pass. We'd flee for safety, then return when calm pretended to be peace. I learned to read every sound, every shift in tone.

My nervous system never knew rest. I still remember what I called the *"smell of fear"*—that heavy air before everything broke again. The chaos shaped who I thought I was long before I had that chance to discover who I truly am, or could be.

One morning, I woke up at my grandparents' house, and the most important person in my world was gone.
The silence that followed didn't soothe—it stung. I tried to make sense of it, feeling small and invisible, wondering what I'd done wrong. It didn't push me into survival mode. I was already there. Carrying the belief that love and safety don't always stay.

Now, through the eyes of the woman I've become, I see what that girl couldn't. That loss wasn't abandonment, it was protection. Sometimes love steps back so strength can step forward, and that moment became the soil where I began to grow. In time, I understood, that my mother didn't leave because she stopped loving me. She left because she loved me.

She believed leaving might give me a better chance. She did what she could with the strength she had. It was never about me being unworthy, it was about her being lost in her own pain that I couldn't see or understand.

Awareness softened me.
Blame became compassion.
Forgiveness didn't erase, it healed.
And, love hadn't left.
It was just loving me differently.

Lost and Learning

School was not my refuge. I was misunderstood and lost, and my grades mirrored the chaos inside me. I started believing the lie that I was the problem. Poor choices piled onto pain until I became someone I barely recognized. Back then, I hated who I was. With no foundation, I was the kind of kid that wasn't supposed to "make it." But my story wasn't one of failure, it was one of resilience. Even in the pain, there was a flicker of something. A quiet, stubborn whisper urging me to keep going, to trust the next step, even when I couldn't see the path ahead. I didn't know it then, but that whisper had a name— "Intuition." It didn't feel spiritual, it felt like survival.

At seventeen, I moved out. No money, no plan, just determination. A knowing that I had to find my own way. Looking back, that was my first act of self-definition.

I stumbled often, but every wrong turn taught me resilience, responsibility, and trust. I learned that mistakes aren't failures, they're redirections toward who you're meant to be. I didn't know how it would unfold, only that I'd figure it out. And somehow, I did.

Remembering My Power

In my early twenties, something extraordinary happened. I stumbled into the world of self-help and empowerment. At first, it was books, stories of people who had overcome impossible odds. Authors who spoke to the part of me that still believed, deep down, that maybe I was meant for more. I didn't have a mentor or a coach. I had books, a journal, and a little yellow fortune of hope. Glimpses of clarity appeared in the middle of confusion, and, piece by piece, those ideas began to change me

I started using gratitude as a lifeline before I understood that it was actually a superpower. I started picturing a future brighter than my past, shifting my mindset from "I can't" to "What if I can?"

Without realizing it, I was laying the foundation for my success. By my mid-twenties, those small shifts compounded, and I went from scraping by, to aligning with my first million. But the real story wasn't about the money— it was about following my intuition. I was unknowingly working with the laws that link assumption, action and transformation. My past no longer defined me.

The secret was to believe differently. Every new choice shaped a new reality. The story I chose to believe became the life I fell in love with.

The Leap

In my early thirties, life carried me into another leap of faith, immigration. Leaving South Africa for Canada was both terrifying and exhilarating. I was starting over again, but this time with more faith, trust, and love.

Every moment— the packing, the paperwork, the flights into the unknown, was proof that together, we were writing a new chapter built on courage and a love strong enough to cross oceans.

My life is the journey, my thinking the map, and my intuition the compass that never fails me. Through it all, family has been my anchor. I've been married for 26 years to the love of my life, and together we've woven a tapestry of memories. Our kids are the heartbeat of everything we do. If childhood taught me resilience, motherhood taught me love.

Fierce. Unconditional. Transformative love.

Ten years ago, after our youngest was born, I sat in meditation, exhausted, but open. Something shifted.
What came through was an intuitive download— a vision showing me how every challenge, every lesson, every heartbreak had been preparing me all along.

What saved me wasn't luck. It was the practices.
Gratitude.
Mindset shifts.
Awareness of energy.
And a deep commitment to serenity— to finding peace in the present moment, no matter the storm.

The same tools that helped me survive could now help others thrive. And with it came a realization that felt like home. What if children didn't have to stumble into self-help in their twenties like I did, but grew up already equipped with these *Hero-skills™*, and the belief that success is a sure thing for them, too?

That's the fire that fuels my mission, to empower the next generation before the world teaches them to doubt themselves. We're not here to raise perfect kids. We're here to raise children who shine from the inside out, who lead with gratitude, wonder with imagination, and meet the world with curiosity and courage. Kids who see mistakes not as flaws, but as invitations to grow— and who rise every time even brighter than before.

Grace in Pause

Even with all the tools I'd gathered, it's easy to slip out of alignment when you stop tending to yourself. When things feel good, you forget the basics. I stopped doing the small things that once kept me grounded.

In my early forties, after years of pouring out without refilling, I could finally feel how out of alignment I was. My body screamed what my soul had long been whispering—*slow down.*

Burnout and Chronic Fatigue hit hard. I was surviving, not living. What first felt like failure became clarity, a wake-up call reminding me to use my "Hero-Skills™", and that the tools only work when you work with them. That season taught me that strength without rest isn't sustainable, and even purpose needs pause. I made the decision, and I began to heal.

From that decision, my purpose didn't fade— it expanded. Today, that defining choice fuels my work with families, leaders who shape the next generation. Children learn not just from what we say, but from who we are. When we lead with possibility, they learn to believe in their own. We are the mirrors that show them what's possible for them and their lives.

Through my work, I help the adults who guide kids embody calm confidence, energy awareness, and emotional presence— so that they can teach and model living with intention.
When children see calm, they learn calm.
When they witness courage, they learn possibility.
And when they feel joy, they remember that it is safe to shine.

Lessons Lived

These aren't theories, they're my lived truths. The blueprint that reshaped my life. A girl who walked through the storm and became the light she was searching for.

One fortune.
Seven words.
And a single choice—to keep moving forward.

Through wounds, rebuilding, heartbreaks, and breakthroughs.
Through highs that tested my faith and rock-bottoms that
stripped me bare so that I could rise stronger.
The ripple was never meant to be mine alone. I see it now — in
my daughters, in families, and in others who carry this work
into their classrooms and homes. I see it in every child who shifts
from "I can't" to "I can't yet." The ripple begins with one,
but it is never meant to end there.

The Laws that Led Me Home

I was living by the Universal Laws long before I knew their
names.
The Law of Attraction guided me when I carried that fortune in
my wallet, believing in something more.
The Law of Cause and Effect shaped my life each time small,
consistent actions created big changes.
The Law of Polarity reminded me that if struggle was real, so
was success, each teaching balance.
And the *Law of Rhythm* showed me that life moves in seasons,
each with its own purpose.
Looking back, I see how every contrast and pause led me here.

They were the invisible framework behind my transformation, the
unseen force that carried me from surviving to serving. These
laws work quietly in the background, just like gravity. You don't
have to believe or even understand them for it to be true. But
when you do, life becomes magical.

You start to trust timing, see patterns, and turn challenges into
breakthroughs. That awareness changed everything for me.
That's why I wove them into my work. If these laws could carry
me from my past to my purpose, imagine what they can do for
the next generation when they learn how to work with them.

I carried that fortune for years, folded, tattered, ink faded. But those words are etched into my being: "Success is a sure thing for you." At seventeen, they felt like a lifeline. At twenty-five, like proof. At thirty-six, like home. And now, in my mid-forties, they feel like a message for every child, parent, and person ready to believe it too.

Redefining Success

Success isn't a destination or a one-size-fits-all. For some, it's financial freedom. For others, it's raising confident kids, nurturing health, or daring to chase a once-impossible dream. At its core, success is the quiet promise that every step taken in faith brings you closer to the life meant for you. Success is certain, not because storms won't come, but because I now know how to stand in them.

There was a time when safety wasn't guaranteed. I lived braced for loss, waiting for the next crack in the foundation, until I learned the truth, I am the foundation. I create my safety. I am the source of the love and stability I once searched for outside of myself. What once felt fragile is now strength, not because life stopped testing me, but because I built the mindset to stand through it. Stability isn't found, it's forged, and I've created a life that I love, not by avoiding uncertainty, but by trusting myself through it.

The Future We Build Together

Let's empower the next generation to rise higher because the adults rose first. Families who build daily habits that ripple through every corner of their lives. Classrooms that nurture resilience instead of fear, and communities that choose connection over competition. We can build this future together, one shift, one consciousness, one smile at a time. The ripple is already in motion. You wouldn't be holding this book if it weren't alive in you already. That whisper that life can be more than survival is proof that you are ready to rise for yourself, and your loved ones. And when doubt creeps in, remember, a beautiful, fulfilling life is waiting for you, if you are bold enough to claim it.

> "Children and adults alike learn through play-
> what better game to master
> than the game of life."
> - Chantelle Sprenger

It is an honour to share the tools that transformed my life with you. Through the *SMILES™* framework, courses, workshops, and *Hero-skills™*, I'll help you build practices that rewire beliefs, spark resilience, and grow confidence. Whether you're a parent raising empowered kids, a teacher bringing calm and purpose to your classroom, or an individual stepping into your next level of growth. I'll walk beside you.

My role is to awaken what's already within you. Your strength. Your inner wisdom. Your ability to create your preferred reality, and the knowing that success can be a sure thing for you too.

Take the leap.
This is your moment.
It begins when you decide.
One single choice can turn the ripple into a wave.

Let's elevate the future together!

Chantelle Sprenger

Chapter 3
The Girl in the Mirror

Opening: Purposed for More

I knew.
I always knew I was purposed for more.

As a little girl at my grandmother's house, I was always a leader when I played —a teacher, a store owner, a speaker. Even back then, I felt chosen. I knew that deep down I had a story to tell. What I didn't realize was that my life would become that story. I would live through pain, betrayal, and brokenness — and then rise from it. I would take the pieces of my pain and use them as a platform to help other women heal.

Being a leader felt natural. Instinctive. I led class projects, held leadership positions throughout school, and even wrote and directed a play with friends in middle school. I had a fire inside me — knowing I was destined for more. But that girl in the mirror back then, though bold and outspoken, wasn't fully confident yet. She didn't know what lay ahead, and she couldn't imagine just how strong she would become.

Part 1: The Escape That Became a Trap

At twenty years old, I was married. If I'm honest, I rushed it. Deep down, I knew it wasn't the best choice, but at the time, it looked like a way out — a rescue from the chaos of my home life. I thought I was stepping into safety, but I was really running straight into another kind of storm.

"Sometimes the girl in the mirror
is the one who saves you."
-Stephanie Harrell

The red flags were there. I ignored them. He was seven years older, more like a father figure than a partner. On the outside, people saw stability — a church leader, a man with a good reputation, and a picture-perfect life. From the outside looking in, we had it all: the house, the cars, successful careers, and the image of a happy family.

Behind closed doors, I was being diminished. I was strong and smart, but I never felt like I was enough. I wanted more, yet I convinced myself that "good enough" would do. I started college as a pre-med, but at his urging, changed my major. That was the first compromise — the moment I gave up my dream.

Part 2: Losing Myself

There came a time when I didn't recognize the woman staring back at me in the mirror. Her eyes looked tired. Her smile was forced. Her spirit — gone.
I used to be vibrant, full of ideas and energy, and dreamt out loud. Somewhere between the yelling, the walking on eggshells, and the pretending, I disappeared.
The abuse wasn't always physical — sometimes it was the silence that screamed the loudest. Looks that made me shrink. Words that cut deep. If I'm honest, I wasn't perfect either. There were times I yelled back. Times I shut down completely. Sometimes I became cold, numb, even mean — just to survive. I wasn't always the victim. Sometimes I was angry. Sometimes I fought to be heard in all the wrong ways. I'd match his energy just to feel like I still had some control. That never worked.
He was the man others respected within the community.
And me? I was the emotional one. The one who "overreacted." The one who was "too sensitive". I started to believe that maybe he was right.

I remember turning to my Pastor. I found myself sitting in his office, tears streaming down my face, and being told to "pray harder."

"God hates divorce," he said.

Part of me believed him. Another part — the quiet, desperate part — started whispering, but does God hate me being broken? Still, I stayed. For the kids. For the church. For the image. And maybe, if I'm really honest, for the version of me that still hoped he'd change.

I had become a shell of who I used to be. And I couldn't tell anymore if I was being destroyed by him…or by the woman I had become, trying to please him.

Part 3: The Breaking Point

The afternoon everything changed was not cinematic. There was no dramatic music, no slow-motion realization. Just me, standing in a room, heart pounding so loud it drowned out everything else. He was angry — angrier than I'd ever seen him. Before I knew it, I was staring down the barrel of a shotgun.

In that instant, everything froze. Time stopped. My breath caught. Somewhere deep inside, a voice whispered, *"So this is it."*

It's strange what you think about when you think you might die. I didn't think about money, or the house, or even him. I thought about my children. I thought about the little girl who used to lead school plays and believed she was meant for more. And I thought, *"What happened to her? How did she end up here?"*

I can't pretend I was perfect — I made my share of mistakes, too. I justified his anger, convinced myself it was love. I had become addicted to the idea of fixing things, of saving someone who didn't want to be saved. In doing that, I had stopped saving myself.

That moment — that gun — snapped me awake. It was like my soul screamed louder than my fear. I thought, *"if I die, it won't be here. It won't be like this. I won't die being small."*

It wasn't bravery at first — it was pure survival. But it was *mine.* In that moment, something inside me changed forever. The woman who had spent years trying to keep the peace finally realized that peace built on silence isn't peace at all — it's a slow death.

That was my breaking point — and my beginning.

Part 4: Choosing Me

Leaving wasn't a clean break — it was messy, painful, and terrifying. I wish I could say I packed my bags and never looked back, but that's not the truth. I left in pieces — emotionally drained, physically exhausted, and spiritually empty.

For years, I had been told that choosing myself was selfish. That good wives stay. That faithful women pray harder. God tests us through suffering. So when I finally left, the guilt almost swallowed me whole.

I kept hearing those voices — church leaders, family, even friends — echoing in my head:

"What will people think?"

"You made your bed, now lie in it."

"He's still your husband."

And underneath it all, another voice — quieter, but steady — whispered, *"You're still here, Stephanie. You still have time. You need to leave him."*

Starting over in my 50s wasn't part of the plan. I was supposed to be settled, stable, secure — not rebuilding my life from scratch. But every morning that I woke up with breath in my lungs, I knew it wasn't too late.

The truth is, I'd been so focused on surviving that I'd forgotten how to live. I didn't know what I liked, what I wanted, or what happiness even felt like. But I knew I couldn't go back.

I started small.

I got up. I made the bed. I looked in the mirror and said something kind — even if I didn't believe it yet. I started treating myself the way I always wished someone else would.

Some days, healing looked like crying in a parked car. Other days, it looked like walking into the gym when every muscle in my body ached from years of carrying emotional weight.

It wasn't glamorous. It wasn't linear. But every single day, I showed up — for *me.*

For the first time in decades, I started to feel something again.

Peace.

Relief.

Hope.

Maybe even a little bit of pride. Because when you've spent your life trying to be enough for everyone else, learning to be enough for yourself feels like freedom.

Part 5: The Healing Journey

Healing didn't come in a rush of light. It came in slow, uneven waves — the kind that crashes over you when you least expect it.

At first, I thought healing meant pretending I was fine. Smiling more. Posting motivational quotes. Acting like the pain was behind me. That was just another mask — I'd worn too many of those already.

The real healing started when I stopped acting strong and let myself *feel weak.* When I stopped asking "*why me*" and started asking "*what now?*"

There were nights when the silence was too loud. I'd lie in bed replaying every bad decision I'd ever made, every red flag I'd ignored, every piece of myself I'd handed away. The shame felt heavy. It wasn't just about what had been done to me — it was about what I had allowed.

And that's what I had to face: my own reflection.

Not with judgment, but with compassion.

I had to forgive myself. Not just for staying too long, but for the choices I made while I was lost — the times I hurt others because I was hurting, the times I settled when I deserved more. Forgiving myself wasn't a one-time thing. It was daily. Sometimes hourly. Slowly, the pieces started to come together. I started reading, journaling, and learning. I joined women's support groups. I worked with trauma coaches. I exercised. I celebrated my small wins.

I built boundaries. Firm ones that protected my energy and peace. I took risks. Said no. Walked away. I chose myself first, every time.

Part 6: Reclaiming Power & Rising Strong

Through this process, I started my coaching business, **Purposeful Mindset** — because mindset controls everything. Your beliefs, your habits, your relationships, your ability to attract what you want. Everything flows from the inside out, and this gave me the purpose I needed to keep going.

The woman I am today is not the same woman who once settled, who once played small to fit into someone else's story.

I am a woman who walked through fire and came out stronger. I created a program, became a certified life coach, and turned my pain into purpose. I no longer silenced myself to make others comfortable.

Part 7: Love as a Bonus

For a long time, I thought love was supposed to complete me. If I prayed harder, did more, looked better, or loved deeper, maybe I'd be worthy of being chosen, of being kept.

Healing taught me something no fairytale ever did: I was already whole.

I dated again, and at first, the same pattern began repeating itself, until I learned to fall in love with ME.

I traveled alone, ate alone, laughed alone. I filled my own cup. I became the person I wanted to attract. When I was truly ready, love arrived. Not to complete me, but to complement me.

He didn't fix me. He celebrated me. He poured into me. But even if he had never come, I was already complete. The love I had been searching for all along was within me.

His love became a bonus. The icing on the cake. I am the cake — strong, steady, and enough on my own.

Part 8: Lessons, Regrets, and Grace

Looking back, there are moments I wish I could undo. Staying too long. Ignoring red flags. Pretending silence was peace. I regret the pain my children felt and all the times I doubted myself.

But I also know this: every choice, misstep, and heartbreak led me here — to clarity, freedom, and strength. The lessons were not punishments. They were guidance. They shaped me into the woman I was always meant to become.

One of the most important lessons I learned: forgive yourself. Forgive others. Release the shame. Honour your growth.

Your voice matters. Speak it, even if it shakes. Share your story, even if no one seems to listen. Courage begets courage.

Remember, it's never too late. No matter your age, your history, or how broken you feel, you can start again. You still have time to rise.

Life is yours. Fill it with courage, grace, and self-love. And when you do, everything else begins to follow.

Conclusion: And So It Is

I was purposed to go through the pain so that I could use it as a platform. I was chosen to rise so that I could help other women rise alongside me. Every scar, every tear, every mistake — they were not signs of failure. They were proof that I was human, that I endured, and that I could transform my life from the inside out. Today, I stand whole. I am enough. I am free. I know this truth with every fiber of my being: worthiness is not something to earn. It is your birthright. You do not have to prove it to anyone — not your family, not your partner, not even yourself.

Believe it before you see it. Live it before you feel it. Step into your power and choose yourself always. Protect your peace, honour your growth, and celebrate every victory — no matter how small.

Life will always challenge you. It will test you. You are capable. You are resilient. No matter your age or where you are in your journey, it's never too late to begin again.

I share my story so that other women can find courage in theirs. So that they know they are not alone, that they are seen, and that they can rise from any pain stronger, wiser, and more radiant than they ever imagined.

And so it is.

Stephanie Harrell

Chapter 4
Visual Frequency Medicine: Born in the Fire

Sensitivity, Trauma & the "Too Much" Lie

I used to think being too sensitive was my downfall. Now, it's my empire.

For most of my life, I carried emotions like weights strapped to my chest—mine, yours, even strangers in the checkout line. I absorbed everything too deeply, too loudly, too much. For decades, I thought that made me broken.

If Phoebe, Monica, and Rachel could combine, it would be me: Phoebe's quirky awkwardness and playful spirit (yes, I snort when I laugh), Monica's obsessive intensity and boldness, and Rachel's flair and her big heart—all rolled into one. Add in ADHD and autism, and you've got a woman who never fit neatly into any box. But once I stopped trying to fix myself and started embracing all of me, I realized my sensitivity wasn't a weakness —it was my superpower.

I'm the girl who cries at movies. The one who senses someone's pain across the room before they ever speak. The one who physically recoils at division—whether racism, bullying, war, or religious separation. I've always wanted everyone to feel loved, safe, and accepted. Even from a young age, my heart was big and I felt a strong calling to help change the world.

Back then, I didn't have language for what was happening inside me. I just knew life felt louder for me than for others—and it was hard. Every high was euphoric, every low cut to the bone. I lived in a constant battle—trying to fix myself, shrink into something more digestible, or desperately trying to make sense of other people's behaviours.

I endured multiple traumas throughout my life, starting at a young age. In middle school, I was bullied so severely that I had to switch schools. I was pushed, elbowed, had tacks put on my chair, tormented at youth groups, and even harassed through phone calls at home. My friends drifted so they wouldn't be targeted too. Nearly every day for two years, I came home in tears. It broke me and my spirit.

I eventually moved from Saskatchewan, Canada, to Montana, USA, to live with my grandparents just across the border. It was supposed to be a fresh start for high school. However, that's when depression, anxiety, severe acne, and IBS began to take root. When even the hint of similar interactions with peers appeared, the trauma response kicked in. I developed an eating disorder 2 years later and went to treatment. I exercised obsessively—up to five hours a day—and starved myself all week, surviving on barely 200 calories a day before binging on weekends to feel "normal" with friends. The need for control consumed me. At my lowest, I weighed only 87 pounds. It's a miracle I survived.

In the years that followed, I attempted suicide twice. I honestly thought my parents would be better without me. Afterwards, someone told me it was a good thing I hadn't succeeded or I'd be burning in hell. She had good intentions, but it pushed me even further from the church I had once longed to belong to and made me ashamed of myself even more.

After high school, I married young. Deep down, I knew during our engagement that I shouldn't get married, but I was terrified of backing out.

We divorced shortly after. The shame of hurting him—and of being so emotionally unwell—stayed with me for two decades. I hated myself for it.

When the Holy Spirit Took Over the Paintbrush

Art was always my therapy. I've been an artist since I could hold a pencil. In hard times, creating was the only thing that quieted the noise in my mind and gave me peace.

After my divorce, I remarried. I fell fast and hard. He was charming, successful, and treated me like a queen. But five years in, everything changed. His occasional drinking became daily and heavy after a traumatic event he developed PTSD from and never sought help for. The marriage became abusive—not physically, but emotionally, mentally, and financially.

Yelling. Swearing. Accusations. Rooms torn apart. Holes punched in walls. He told me what to think, controlled the money, and isolated me from friends. I was so conditioned that when his family defended me, I couldn't even recognize the abuse. My stepson, who was severely mentally unwell, made the home unsafe as well. I feared for my life.

To add to it, in my 30s, I lost the use of my dominant arm after a blood draw that hit a nerve and tendon. Eventually, I was diagnosed with CRPS (Chronic Regional Pain Syndrome). The pain was relentless. Doctor after doctor told me there was no cure. That it would only get worse.

So, I gave up.

I donated all my canvases, paints, and craft supplies. The grief was crushing—my independence, my art, even carrying my five-year-old son—all felt stolen.

And with my arm injury, I was completely dependent on others—sometimes unable to tie my shoes, cut my food, or wash my hair. Looking back now, I can see how the energy and mindset I carried from early trauma kept drawing in more of the same. Pain layered upon pain—mental, emotional, physical, spiritual.

At times, my life felt like hell on Earth.

Ten years into our marriage, as ashamed as I was to be facing another divorce—and as terrifying as it felt—I finally left. And the moment I did, something unexpected happened: I felt free. There were still many unknowns and healing ahead, but for the first time in a long time, I felt hope.

Not long after, I found myself in another relationship. He love-bombed me right away—told me he'd been in the Marines and would protect me when I was scared. He cooked every meal, said all the right things, and knew exactly how to make me feel seen and safe. I was an easy target.

From the outside, it was obvious to others what was happening —but I was too broken to see it clearly. That's exactly why he chose me. He was a skilled con artist, complete with the stories and receipts to sell his lies. But even in that dark chapter, something sacred happened.

One morning over breakfast, I felt the Holy Spirit move through me for the first time. It was undeniable. Something shifted deep within me. After years of longing to know God, I finally *felt* Him— and I believed. The man I was with used this moment to his advantage. He twisted scripture to manipulate me, using the Bible as a weapon to control and shame me. But it didn't work for long.

My eyes opened. I kicked him out and promised myself I would stay single for two years. I needed to find myself again—and follow where this newfound faith would lead.

My arm miraculously healed.

My mind cleared.

The heaviness lifted.

Doors began to open.

Everything changed—just like that.

When I started painting again, it wasn't just art anymore. It became my devotion to God. I began every session with gratitude—for my health, my supplies, my space, etc.. I'd play a song on repeat and pray the entire time. Each painting carries that song's frequency—the title is written on the back so you can listen as you view the piece. This is why my art isn't just something beautiful to look at.

Visual Frequency Medicine.

Turning raw emotion and experiences into art is the medicine—and the Holy Spirit moves through each brushstroke as a tangible frequency you can see and feel. My creations are living prayers, designed to elevate the energy of you, your home, and everyone who enters it. As someone who has experienced so much darkness that was meant to destroy me, I now realize that I am a living testimony to God's love. I'm here to share His light through art that will speak to your soul and activate or deepen your faith.

I believe anyone can use art as a tool for healing. It doesn't matter how it looks—it's about what you feel. Play with colour, texture, charcoal, and markers. Experiment with brushes, sponges, sticks, and your fingers. Paint with your non-dominant hand. Paint blindfolded. Follow your intuition. Let go. See what happens.

That's why I teach others to paint—not just as a creative outlet, but as a way to connect with God, with others, and with the truest, rawest version of themselves.

Creating Everyday Tools for the Spirit-Led Woman

Within the first year of painting again, I sold over 26 originals to collectors across Canada, the U.S., and the U.K. It was a dream come true. All I did was follow the nudge, create from the heart, and share the meaning behind each piece—and it resonated. As my art reached more hands and homes, I felt called to bring that same intention into everyday goods.

Imagine this:

You rise early. The house is still. You walk into your kitchen, open the cupboard, and reach for your favourite mug—the one that reminds you that everything will be okay. Or maybe it's the one that whispers:

Follow the joy.
Give yourself grace.
Breathe.

I've designed mugs, each with a specific intention.

Not just for sipping,
but for centering,
and for empowering.

Alongside them are my sacred soul journals, candles, and note cards—each infused with care and frequency that uplifts.

They're not just pretty things.
They're visual prayers. Anchors. Reminders.

Here's the truth: We are all artists of our lives, and we get to choose how we paint it—the colours, the strokes, and the medium. So why not make it sacred?

From New Age to New Creation

Ultimately, getting to know Christ is what allowed me to truly love and accept myself— deeply and completely. That in itself was a long road, especially after the pain and abuse I'd endured multiple times in life.
As women, we're taught to carry the world's weight and stay quiet. To hold our pain, to appear strong, to shrink when we feel too much, and look pretty while doing it all. But the truth is—we were never meant to do it alone.

We have to *feel* it to *release* it.
Art helps us access that truth.
It moves emotion. It connects us.
But faith—that's what anchors us.

I am a trailblazer—and if you're reading this, you likely are too. I recently walked away from New Age practices and Reiki.

Becoming a Reiki Master a year after my profound healing once felt aligned and made sense as a next step. It gave me a framework to use my intuition, serve others, and serve God.
My gifts increased, I discovered new ones, and I believed I was helping people heal. It was empowering. But if I'm honest, it also fed my ego—to connect with spirits and to receive messages, to feel "chosen" and "special".

Yes, Reiki and quantum healing helped me process trauma.
Conscious manifestation and witchcraft helped me attract many things that I wanted.
But there were consequences.

Over time, my health began to decline again. I was anxious, emotional, and constantly trying to "protect my energy."

It felt like a dark night of the soul that never ended. I became hypersensitive, isolated, and unknowingly, I slowly drifted away from scripture, from church, from Christian music, and from Jesus.

I thought I was following God's will.
But now I see—it was deception. A counterfeit light.

Little did I know that when I painted a commissioned piece called The Great Return—about the Second Coming of Christ, a seed was planted. Months later, I heard a voice say,"Just talk to Jesus." So I did. And in true Jade fashion—I tested it.

From that moment, everything changed. My health improved again. My relationship with my boyfriend deepened. I published my first book. I found my dream studio and I am opening a gallery, boutique and event center. Blessings began pouring in.

Since then, I've fully returned to Christ—and it's the most incredible feeling of love, safety, and peace I've ever known. He is merciful and will leave the 99 to find the 1 lost sheep.

Now, I'm off the hamster wheel of "spiritual striving" and letting Jesus take the wheel instead.

No more Reiki. It opens doors you can't control.
No more moon ceremonies, crystals, or burning sage to manifest.

No more channeling spirits or obsessing over protecting my energy.
Just Him.
Because after everything I've lived through, I can say with full conviction:
Jesus is the only way.

And now, I can't wait to see what He does in me, through me, and through my brand—Jade Breanne Collective.
I had already written this chapter once, but after this divine awakening, I knew I had to rewrite it.

You are the artist—and life is your canvas.

At the end of this chapter, I invite you to visit my website and explore my original artwork, prints, and goods. See what speaks to your soul—because if something resonates, it's for a reason.

With all my heart and vibrant possibilities,

Jade Breanne Olszewski

Chapter 5
THE LONG ROAD HOME

The Long Road Home

I was running with everything I had. Legs burning, chest pounding, breath ragged. Sweat poured down my face as I stumbled forward, screaming, reaching with all the desperation in my body. Just a few feet ahead, my mother stretched her hands out toward me from the open trunk of a moving car. Our fingertips nearly touched, but never met. The car sped faster. My legs turned to jelly, my lungs gasped for air, my heart hammered so hard it felt like it might burst. And then, she was gone.

Out of sight, I collapsed to the ground in a flood of sweaty tears, fear, and defeat. And just as the weight of it consumed me, I jolted awake. It was a nightmare that haunted me every single night for years. A nightmare that clung to me until I finally faced the truth I'd been carrying in silence, until I spoke out about my uncle sexually abusing me. The suppression, the inner struggle, the fear, shame, and guilt that I had been avoiding were the energy feeding this nightmare.

For years, I thought the nightmare was just my mind torturing me. But what I didn't realize was that it was my body, my nervous system, screaming for me to pay attention. It was the unspoken pain, the buried memories, the suppression of my emotions that I had locked deep inside, clawing to be seen.

The day I finally spoke my truth out loud to my mother, everything shifted. It was as if my soul had been holding its breath for decades and finally exhaled. That moment marked the beginning of my healing and the end of the nightmare, raw, terrifying, and liberating all at once.

That was the true beginning of my healing journey. For years, I sat across from counselors and therapists, talking and retelling my story, searching for relief, but no matter how many sessions I attended, the memories clung to every cell in my being. The pain sat heavy in my chest. The weight of it all, never truly lifted.

Back then, I didn't realize the same things I was trying so desperately to release were not just in my mind, they were buried deep in my body.
Every word I spoke in therapy scratched the surface, but it never reached the root. My nervous system was locked in survival, constantly bracing, never feeling safe.

The weight of carrying pain that I couldn't release was unbearable. No matter how much I tried to push it down or forget about it, it left me feeling hollow, like a shell of myself, empty and unworthy of love. But so desperately wanting to be loved, wanting to be seen, wanting to be validated.

What I now understand is that we don't attract what we want, we attract what we are, and what we embody.
And at that time, I was living in shame, drowning in guilt, swallowed by fear, and sadness and starved of self-love.
Inevitably, our outer world mirrors our inner world and whatever is going on inside of us, is reflected outside of us. By natural laws, I found myself surrounded by relationships, experiences, and people who only expanded and reflected the pain I already carried.

I became a master of pretending, not trusting myself, a people pleaser, bending myself to prove my worth, self-sacrificing, smiling on the outside, while on the inside I was aching with sorrow and silently screaming.

It was exhausting wearing a mask so convincing that even I sometimes believed it but deep down I knew something had to change. In my disconnection, I was making choices from the raw aches of my wounds. I attracted and married a man who was also vibrating on these low frequencies, he tore me down and every day with him felt like I was slipping further and further away from myself. I numbed the hollow ache with drugs and alcohol, chasing relief but instead it unleashed chaos, violent fights, broken glass, screaming voices.

The pain I tried to bury only grew louder, darker, sharper.

There came a point when the darkness wrapped around me so tightly that I couldn't breathe. I truly believed there was no way out. Death seemed like the only door, the only way to silence the torment that clawed at me day in and day out.

And then, my three children.

Their faces would flash before me in those darkest moments. Their innocent eyes. Their small, trusting hands, their laughter that deserved joy, not the echo of my suffering. The thought of them growing up carrying my pain stopped me from driving off the bridge that I regularly rehearsed in my mind. They were my fragile thread of hope, the last light I could still see.

The final breaking point came when my son called my mother to come over after a violent fight with my husband. She looked me dead in the eyes, her voice steady, her love fierce. "If you don't leave this marriage, I will take your children from you."

Her words sliced through the fog, cutting straight to my core. In that instant I knew I had no choice left. I had to fight, I had to leave. Trembling but resolute, I walked away from the marriage. My children and I moved in with my mother and her husband, where we spent the next couple of years.

Their home became our refuge, steady, safe, and overflowing with love. It was exactly what we all needed during such a fragile and uncertain time.

Within that environment of love and encouragement, something inside of me began to shift. The suffocating weight of the past started to loosen its grip, and for the first time in years, I felt the faintest relief. It was like glimpsing a silver light after being trapped in the darkness.

That light sparked curiosity. I began to wonder: what else is out there? What else is possible for me, for my children, for the life I've yet to live? Those questions stirred a deep reconnection with my heart and soul, nudging me toward paths I had never explored before.

I sought out mentorship and invested in coaching. I immersed myself in training and programs, learning to both practice and facilitate breath-work and somatic healing.

I learned healing is a paradox, to truly heal, we must allow ourselves to feel. We must fully acknowledge and process the pain that accompanied our trauma, rather than trying to think our way through it.

Healing does not happen in the mind alone, it happens through the body. By engaging in somatic practices like breath-work, movement and sound to create space within the body to feel, release and let go of what I had been holding inside my body. As my body released, with these practices my mind softened, returning to my natural regulated state of ease and safety.

Somatics was the missing piece of my healing journey, one that revealed itself only after I stepped away from the chaos that had kept my nervous system in constant survival mode. Once I created space and safety within and around me, my body finally felt ready to speak. I began to uncover layers of emotion I had not even realized I was holding. Each somatic release became a doorway back to myself, a remembrance of my wholeness, a reclaiming of my power and a deep exhale into freedom.

I allowed myself to be stretched by new perspectives, ones that expanded my awareness and dismantled old beliefs about who I thought I was and what life was supposed to look like. Little by little, breath by breath, I began to step out of mere survival and into the deeper journey of self-discovery.

I started taking radical responsibility for my choices, my healing, and my future. The identity of the victim that I had worn like a badge of honour for so long began to fall away, and in its place, I began to glimpse the strength of the woman I was becoming.

I did not yet know how far this journey would take me, but the first cracks of transformation were beginning to show. And what lay on the other side was more powerful than I could have ever imagined.

I was remembering a deeper truth that everything is energy. We live in an energetic universe, and our thoughts and emotions carry frequencies that shape the reality we experience.

We are the cause behind the effect, and what we send out always returns to us. With this awareness, I began to speak words of love and acceptance into myself. I offered myself grace and compassion, and I chose to focus on possibilities rather than problems.
I came to see that everything in my life had unfolded with purpose, it was happening for me, not to me.

The pain and suffering I had endured were not punishments but catalysts, strengthening me, stretching me, and guiding me into growth and evolution.

Those experiences prepared me to stand now as a sacred and safe space holder for truth, healing and transformation, walking beside others on their own paths of healing and transformation. I had to experience the depths of darkness in order to now be the light.

As I deepened into this truth, spirituality became my compass. I remembered that we are spiritual beings having a human experience, and that our souls intentionally chose this path.

I began to understand that my role is to restore what was once forgotten, to bring back the missing codes of remembrance through my voice, my presence, my work, my teachings. I am here to help humanity awaken to the truth that has always lived within them.

Some esoteric traditions speak of the great silence, a time when humanity, and even parts of the cosmos, lost connection to the original frequencies of truth, love and creation. I now know that part of my purpose is to bridge the gap, to help restore what was lost during that long silence, and guide people back home to themselves.

Every time I hold sacred space, guide breathwork or speak truth, I reinstate those codes. I am restoring what others have lost touch with in themselves. Humanity has forgotten its wholeness and my work, breath-work, coaching and retreats is literally helping people remember who they truly are, coming home to themselves. The missing codes are not abstract, they are states of love, safety and authenticity that I help them unlock.

As I embraced this calling, I understood that every challenge, every fracture, and every silence, illusion and distortion had been part of the greater remembering. Nothing was wasted, and nothing was ever truly lost.

The pain became wisdom, the darkness became light, the disconnection became the very doorway back to connection. And now, I stand in this truth, not just for myself, but for all who are ready to remember.

So if you, like me, have ever felt broken, lost, alone or disconnected, know this: these experiences are not your ending, they are your becoming.

They are shaping you, refining you, helping you remember and guiding you back to who you have always been. You are whole, you are worthy and you are powerful.

Beloved, keep trusting and loving yourself.
Keep opening to receive the vast power that lives within your breath, your body, and your spirit.
With every inhale, receive the infinite possibility of life.
With every exhale, release what no longer belongs.
Let breath, movement and sound carry you back into the truth and essence of your being.

You are the remembrance.

You are the light.

You are the power.

You are the home you have been searching for. Welcome home beloved sou!

If this story has touched something within you, if you feel the whisper of your own awakening calling you home, know that your healing is possible too.

You don't have to walk this path alone. To deepen your transformation and explore how I can serve and support you on your journey back to remembrance, I invite you to visit my website and connect with me on social media. Together, we can continue to release, rise and return to the truth of who you are, free, powerful and fully alive!

Chantelle Miller

Chapter 6
My Testimony
My Victory

My Intentions

I feel called to share my story so that others living in silent pain may find their voice. My prayer is that you will have the courage to love yourself the way others love you-to trust and know how amazing you are, just as you were created. Beautiful as you are! My hope is that, as you read these words, you will see pieces of your own journey reflected in mine. You, too, can be an overcomer. You can find the happiness you were always meant to feel and receive in this life. Through self-love and forgiveness, you can elevate your existence.

Our stories are more connected than we realize. We live parallel lives, often without knowing it. And in that parallel journey, there is power, the power of recognition, of transformation, and of hope. Life is meant to be fun, and sharing our experiences opens the doorway to that truth.
Writing and speaking about my transformation allows me to live in complete gratitude and joy. Each time I reflect on my journey, I grow stronger. My wish is for everyone to taste that same joy and to live and breathe it daily.

Living a Double Life

For years, I lived what I call a *double life*. On one side was the Margaret people knew and admired: vibrant, smiling, full of energy. She was loved, successful, and appeared to be thriving. People often told me, "You're so happy. You have such a beautiful life." And in many ways, they were right. I did have a beautiful, blessed life. I was loved by everyone **but myself.**
But there was another Margaret, the one nobody saw. She hid behind the mask, living in silent pain. She carried a void she couldn't name, an ache that was constant yet invisible.

I could be in a room full of people, surrounded by love, and still feel lonely. This contradiction was confusing and heavy, and along with it came guilt and shame. How could someone who had so much to be grateful for feel so empty inside? I asked myself this question countless times, never finding an answer. Instead, I became an expert at pretending. My disguise was so flawless that I even fooled myself.

The Breaking Point

There comes a moment in life when the mask cracks. No matter how carefully you've held it together, the truth beneath demands to be seen.

For me, that moment came quietly, yet powerfully. I remember sitting alone one evening, feeling the weight of my own unhappiness pressing down so heavily that I could no longer escape it. I realized I had been living for everyone else's vision of me— the Margaret who made others smile, who held everything together, who seemed unshakable. But the inner Margaret was crumbling.

It was in that low place that I faced a choice: to keep living in silent suffering or to finally fight for my own happiness. Fear whispered that it was easier to stay hidden, to keep performing the role that everyone loved.

My mind told me to
play safe and stay safe,
but my spirit cried out for — **FREEDOM.**

I chose to listen to that cry. With trembling courage, I admitted to myself that I was not okay. That was the beginning of my healing- not pretending, not covering up, but facing my truth.

Facing the Silence Going Within

I had to finally face my fears. But what were they? Where were they rooted? When did they begin?

So many questions. So much confusion.

I had lived in denial for so long that I lost sight of what was reality and what was fantasy. I had become a master at hiding my emotions. No one ever noticed I was in pain—how could they? I never allowed myself to show vulnerability.

I was the one everyone turned to for strength. I convinced myself that if I showed weakness, they would no longer love me. My biggest fear was disappointing others. If I thought I would hurt someone I couldn't live with myself- especially those I loved so dearly. My self-worth depended on how other people perceived me. I lost touch with my own self-love.

This was no performance. I wasn't playing a role on stage. This was my life— my pain.

Inside, my little girl was screaming for love. She wanted to be seen, to be heard, to be held, to feel safe. She had been on her own for so long that she became numb. She lost her voice. The greatest tragedy was not what others did to me, but the silence I forced upon myself.

Using my voice has always been painful. I ignored my own needs to make others happy. I really didn't have any self-worth. I was there for everyone else offering love, guidance, and safety. It was my gift. But I could not offer it to myself.
At the height of my outer success, I was at my lowest inside. Many nights ended in trauma and uncontrollable tears, fear

and loneliness. And then, at age sixty-two, my world shattered.

No one knew the depth of what I was feeling. Not my family. Not my husband. Not my friends, colleagues, or students. I wanted to run as far as I could and never look back. I was on the verge of a nervous breakdown. Actually, I was in the flow of one.

The pain was unbearable. My stomach burned like a circle of fire. My heart burst open. And there, standing before me, were all my years of hiding raw, exposed, undeniable.

It was horrific. The scariest moment of my life.

And yet what I thought was my undoing became the greatest gift I had ever been given.

The Gift

How could something so horrifying…ever be a gift? I didn't know it then. But my breakdown was my breakthrough. My collapse became my victory. I took a leap of faith. I invested in myself. In my self-care. In my healing. I was led divinely to the right people, the ones who held the lanterns as I walked through the dark. My angels from God. I thank him for sending me these souls, the anchors in my storm, who gave me the courage to stay firmly rooted in my healing.

For the first time, I broke the silence. I let the beast out. I am thankful to my partner, my husband, whose love became a sacred gift in my healing- a reflection of God's grace reminding me that I was never alone.

I realized…My silence had never been a weakness. It was my protection. It was my strength. I learned to give myself grace.

I whispered to myself: *"It's okay my love to not be okay."*

And slowly, I took back my power. The inner work was raw. It was painful. It shook my soul.
It emptied me out, so light could enter again. I unearthed the emotions I had buried since childhood. I began to love myself… the way others had always loved me. I began to see and respect the real me, the joyful me-the beautiful me who had been locked away.

Day after day, I studied my own being. I brought awareness to my feelings. I allowed myself to *feel* them all. Because we must *feel to heal*. Even the ugly ones. Even the painful ones. I stopped hiding from them and running away from them.

There were days I cried until nothing was left. For days I was weak, numb, curled up in bed. So sick with grief that my body shut down. I passed out and I woke up in a hospital bed.
The doctors couldn't find anything wrong.

But I knew,
This was the purging
This was the release
This was healing

The frightened, insecure me was fading away.
So that the authentic me could finally be born. Like a snake shedding its skin, I was making room for new growth. And with time, the pieces of my life's puzzle began to fall into place.

The greatest gift I received was awareness.
Once I became aware I could never go back.
I could never pretend again.
The days of pretending…were over.

Anchors of My Healing

Two anchors guided me through my transformation: God and Dance, Divine Movement

My faith in the Divine became my lifeline. In my weakest moments, I turned to God, and I felt His presence reminding me that I was never alone. Trusting in Divine love gave me the strength to keep going when doubt crept in. My faith became the anchor that steadied me when waves of loneliness and fear tried to pull me under.

Faith had always been part of my life, but during my healing it became something deeper it became my medicine. I thank God for my beautiful mother who taught me the love of God from childhood.

The stronger my faith is,
the stronger my life is.

My love for dance has always been a blessing in my life, a divine gift, however I didn't truly understand just how profound this gift was, and still is, on my journey. When I danced, I released what words could not hold. I was able to move energy and let go of feelings and emotions that were trapped in my soul.

Each movement became a prayer, each beat of the music an invitation to let go of pain. Movements allowed me to step into authenticity, to feel joy again, to reconnect with the little girl inside me who once danced freely without fear. Dance allowed me to fill my emptiness with confidence and joy.
These two powerful anchors, God and dance carried me back to myself. They reminded me that healing is not only possible, it is promised when we open our hearts to it.

No Easy Journey

As I write my story,
I realize…opening myself to the world is no easy task.

To relive the horror of my transformation…
is to feel it again.
But this time,
I am shifted into someone stronger, healthier, happier. Giving myself grace and love.

To you, my reader
I want you to know the truth.
How vulnerable I felt.
How weak and ashamed
How heavy the pain sat inside me.

It takes courage to reveal it.
It takes trust to believe that no matter what occurs…All is, and will be well.

The events I walked through were some of the most frightening moments of my life. Moments I thought would break me.
But they didn't.

Instead, they made me.
What I believed would be my demise was, in fact… my rebirth.

And this,
this right here—
is the sweet spot of my story.
The honey in the tea.

Because even in the darkest journey,
All is well.
And I am living proof of it.

This is not the end of my story. It has only just begun.
My life is a work in progress; there is so much more to express.
Every day, I rise.
Every day, I heal.
Every day, I aspire to become the person God has created me to be.

And one thing is for certain.
My happiness is worth every single step I take.

So now, I know…
forward is the only way for me.

My Victory

Today, I live with gratitude and joy. I no longer hide behind the mask of silent pain. Instead, I embrace the wholeness of who I am. My voice is no longer silent.
My testimony is living proof that transformation is real.

I share this story not to dwell on the struggle, but to magnify the victory. Because if healing and freedom is possible for me, they *are* possible for you too.

To all the beautiful people reading this, my wish is that you embody these words and know how worthy you are of all of it. We were not created to live half-lives. We were not made to carry emptiness in silence.

We were not made to play small. We were made for joy. We were made for love. We were made to rise. Your happiness is worth fighting for. And if I could do this, then so can you. Trust your intuition if you are seeking more, more is seeking you.

And here is the beauty: when even one person dares to believe these words, when one heart takes its first step toward healing—
my victory multiplies!
So, I pause my story here (for now) … with the lyric that carries my spirit from the song titled, *I Made It*:
"I'm coming out the other side stronger, one foot in front of another."

Hands still raising … heart still praising …

I MADE IT. I MADE IT. I MADE IT.

Life is meant to be lived in joy. And you, yes, you, are worthy of that joy.

*"This is not the end of my story.
This victory is only a glimpse, the real story has just begun."*

So, come walk with me into what comes next.....

With Divine Love,

Margaret Tapogna Gatzonis

Chapter 7

When the Body Screams What the Heart Can't Say

When the Body Screams What the Heart Can't Say

I remember rushing to the hospital, my heart pounding so violently it felt as if it might split wide open inside my chest. Sadness poured over me like a tidal wave, pulling me under before I could catch my breath. Fear clung to my throat with icy fingers, and anxiety screamed through my veins like a siren. Each beat of my heart was a drum of panic, echoing against my ribs like thunder in a storm.

The elevator ride to palliative care seemed endless. The cables hummed with an almost mocking calm, while my insides twisted with dread. Each floor that passed felt like another stone pressing onto my chest, dragging me deeper into a reality I wasn't ready to face. When the doors finally opened, I stepped into a hallway that seemed to stretch for miles. Dimly lit, shadows clung stubbornly to the walls as though the light itself didn't want to intrude. The air was thick with disinfectant and something heavier—sorrow, grief, and the unmistakable presence of death.

My footsteps echoed faintly, yet the sound seemed swallowed by the weight of silence. Each step grew slower, heavier, as if I were being pulled back by an invisible hand. My breath came shallow, my legs dragged forward unwillingly, as though my body already knew what my heart refused to accept. That hallway was more than walls and floor—it was a passage between life as I had known it and the heartbreak waiting at its end.

Finally, at the farthest end, I reached the door of my grandmother's room. I froze, standing outside her door, my hand trembling just above the handle. The silence behind it pressed against me, louder than any sound I had ever heard. The truth rose like bile in my throat. Once I opened this door, denial would be gone. Reality would take over. Looking back now, I realize that the doorway was more than just wood and hinges—it was the threshold between who I was as a granddaughter, and who I would become without her. It was the first of many doors, grief would force me to open. I drew in a deep breath that felt like I was inhaling glass and pushed the door open.

Grandma lay in her bed, so tiny and fragile, she seemed almost swallowed by the cot itself. Her skin was pale, stretched thin over delicate bones. Her eyes were tinged with yellow, her body weakened to the point of breaking. It looked like time itself was slipping out of her veins. And yet, when her eyes found mine, her whole face lit up. She smiled—oh, what a smile. Radiant, beautiful, filled with love. It was as if her spirit, though bound to a failing body, had risen for one last moment to remind me that love outlasts even death.

I pulled a chair close to her bedside and sat, struggling to hide the storm inside me. My throat ached, swollen, with tears burning behind my eyes. "Grandma," I whispered, my voice trembling, "you can't leave me."

The dam broke. Tears poured from me uncontrollably, streaking down my cheeks faster than I could wipe them away. "Please, Grandma, I sobbed. Don't leave me here. You can't. I need you."

Her hand reached for mine, frail but still warm. Her voice was soft, steady despite the weakness of her body. "Ashley, it's okay, my girl. Everything is going to be okay." I shook my head violently, choking on my grief. "No, Grandma. No, it won't. They already don't like me. When you're gone, I won't have anyone. Please don't go. Please."
She squeezed my hand gently, her eyes holding mine with a

strength that defied her frailty. "Ashley, you will be okay. Everyone loves you. And I need you to promise me something." I leaned closer, desperate to catch every syllable, afraid her words might slip away like sand through my fingers.

"I want you and your sister to always be there for each other," she said. "Promise me, no matter what, you will get along and you will be there for one another."

My vision blurred with tears, but I nodded. "Okay, I promise. I'll always be there for her. I promise you."

Even now, I can still feel the weight of that promise. It wasn't just a vow to her—it was a vow to myself, to carry her love forward in the only way I could. Promises made in grief have a way of shaping who we are for the rest of our lives.

Those words were her final gift to me, my last vow to her. I knew then those were our last moments. I said my goodbyes, memorizing every line on her face, every crease carved by laughter and love. I knew it would be the last time I would see her alive.

At the time, I was pregnant with my youngest daughter, Danika. A new heartbeat growing inside me, while another, who I loved the most, was fading away. Life and death crossing paths. The weight of that irony was unbearable.

Day by day, week by week, I tried to stay strong after Grandma passed. I visited Grandpa whenever I could, but life with four kids often left me stretched thin. Still, every chance I had, I went.

Grandpa had a way of watching the kids with half amusement, and half exasperation. Whenever my boys got into mischief, he'd point with a chuckle, "Watch them, haha." His eyes always glimmered, even as his body grew weaker.

But less than a year later, Grandpa let go too. He had already endured so much—years before, a stroke, and then a colon cancer diagnosis. Yet he fought with a courage that humbled me, holding on with stubborn strength. After Grandma died, something inside of him broke. His heart couldn't keep beating without hers beside it. Deep down, I knew it was only a matter of time before he would follow her.

The funerals crushed me. Funerals always had. Each one felt like a shovel digging deeper into the hollow space in my chest.

Grief doesn't just take the people you love—it takes versions of you too. The granddaughter, the child, the believer in forever. Each funeral stripped away a layer of who I thought I was, leaving someone new and raw behind.

Through my twenties, I threw myself into motherhood. I did what I thought I was supposed to do—be a mom, raise my children, build a life. The relationship I was in at the time felt tolerable at first, but soon it soured. Addiction had its claws deep in my partner, twisting him into someone cruel. Emotional and mental abuse became part of the daily rhythm. The yelling never seemed to stop, and at times it hovered dangerously close to crossing lines with the children.

I felt trapped, a bird in a cage with the door wide open but my wings weren't strong enough to fly. With no job, no money, no safety net, I couldn't muster the courage to leave. Fear of the unknown held me prisoner.

But my mom saw me. She saw through the lies I told myself, through the façade of surviving. One day she looked me straight in the eyes, her voice sharp with truth and love.

"Ashley, you know you're never going to get half. You know he's always going to throw it in your face that he pays for everything. Why don't you leave and start over?"

Her words struck like lightning—sudden, undeniable, illuminating a path I had been too scared to see. That was my cue. My lifeline.

With nothing but my courage and my children, I left. We piled into my green Jeep with only a few clothes and personal belongings. No money, no plan, no safety net. Just a desperate leap into freedom.

It's strange how courage doesn't always feel like bravery. Sometimes it feels like terror, like driving away, hands shaking, no map, only the whisper and knowing that you deserve better. But I see now—that is what bravery really is.

Homeless, we couch-surfed at friends' houses. It was hard— excruciating—but necessary.

That's when my own addiction began. I didn't want to feel. I didn't want to endure the grief of losing my grandparents, the failure of my relationship, the loneliness of being uprooted.

Drugs became my numbness, my escape from reality. Foolish, yes. Destructive, absolutely. But in those moments, it felt like the only way to breathe.

Eventually, I secured a low-income house. I waitressed to scrape by, balancing trays and survival.

I decided to go back to school. I wanted to be somebody. I wanted to be a nurse. After losing my grandparents, helping others felt like a way to heal myself.

But my body betrayed me. Crashes, exhaustion, an unrelenting sickness. I went to doctor after doctor, desperate for answers. Every test came back empty, unanswered.

"You worry too much," one doctor said with a dismissive smile. "It's probably just anxiety."

Meanwhile, my addiction worsened. School slipped through my fingers until I finally dropped out. Subconsciously, I knew why: I didn't want to feel. Not the grief of losing my grandparents, not the weight of the failed relationship, not the crushing pressure of life itself.
Life carried on,
but it spiraled fast.

Then came the blow that shattered me: Mom was diagnosed with lung cancer.

It hit like a tsunami, a wave that swallowed everything in its path. The thought of losing her was unbearable. I had already lost half my heart with my Grandparents; now I faced losing the other half.

Grief teaches you how fragile life is, but nothing prepares you for watching someone you love slip away piece by piece. Love makes us fierce, but it also makes us helpless. That's the cruel balance.
My addiction worsened tenfold. Mom knew I wasn't okay. We all did. I desperately wanted to be there for her, but I couldn't. Not in the condition I was in. The guilt, the shame, the sadness— it crushed me.

Each time I left her side, I went home and cried until my body ached. At night, I prayed silently, begging God to take me instead. To give me her pain. She didn't deserve this. "God, Please, take me." I'd pray.

But God did not take me. And she only grew sicker. On November 24th, 2019, my world collapsed. The message from my dad landed like a blade: Your mother has passed. I fell to my knees, gasping for air, drowning in a panic attack. The walls closed in, the floor dropped beneath me, and grief swallowed me whole.

It was six days before my birthday.

That birthday never felt like the beginning of another year—it felt like the end of the world I knew. Grief has a way of marking time differently: before the loss, and after it. That day was the line that split my life in two.

On November 30th, I went to buy drugs, trying to outrun the tidal wave of pain. But when the baggie was handed to me, I froze. Staring at it, disgust rising inside me. This is the problem. Right here. This is the fucking problem.

It was a lightbulb moment, sudden and piercing. I realized I didn't want to numb the pain anymore—I wanted to feel it, to face it, to change. I looked at my children and thought of my family. Those gone and those still here. I thought of the good memories, the bad ones, the grief, the love. Losing my grandparents and my mother had carved wounds so deep I thought they'd never heal, but they also lit a fire in me. I knew then that this had to change. Now.
So, I began. Small steps at first. Weights. Running. Changing my diet.

One day, one week, one month at a time. "Ashley, you can do this. You've got this!" A tiny voice whispered inside me, kept me going. Recovery wasn't easy, but it was necessary. I reached out to my dad to apologize for not being there for Mom. I told him I was different now, that I had changed. His response was cautious: "Okay, we'll see where this goes." Those words were enough. More than rejection, more than silence. They were a beginning, and I clung to them like a lifeline.

I healed— slowly, painfully, but I healed.
Until the next storm arrived. Years of unexplained illness, dismissal from doctors, misdiagnoses, and finally the truth: endometriosis.

By May 2025, after endless waiting, I was finally scheduled for surgery. My uterus had grown thirteen inches, pressing against my bowels, twisting my insides into chaos. When I woke up after surgery, writhing in pain, the doctor came to my bedside. He shook my hand and said, "You're a strong girl."

At that moment, I saw her—my grandmother's face flashing before me as I heard his words. I felt her presence in the strength I had found, in the survival as I clawed my way back from grief and addiction. And, I knew the truth I had been searching for all along: love carries us through. Even when half the heart is gone, its echo remains, urging us to keep going.

I've spent my entire life searching for acceptance — ever since I was a little girl. I just wanted to be seen and loved for who I truly am. It's taken me a long time, but now, at forty, I've finally realized something beautiful: I am more than enough.
I no longer need anyone else's approval or validation. I accept and deeply love myself, my differences, my authenticity, my uniqueness. I am more than enough.

If you've felt these same struggles, or if you're simply curious about how my life continues to unfold beyond this chapter, I'd love for you to join me on my journey.

I still have an undiagnosed auto immune disease, which I believe to be lupus. There is a butterfly rash on my face. I am now being told I have a suspected genetic condition, called Elhers-Danlos syndrome (DLS). There are 13 subtypes of this gene.

My story is far from over — and maybe, in some way, it connects with yours too.

Ashley Crawford

Chapter 8
Choosing Life

Before the Storm

Before everything changed, my life looked beautiful from the outside, almost picture-perfect. I went to an all-girls private school and had a group of best friends I swore would be in my life forever. On paper, I had it all: a loving family, incredible siblings, a roof over my head, food on the table, and the freedom to choose any path for my future.

But inside, I couldn't see any of it. I struggled with depression and anxiety so badly that I was blind to the beauty surrounding me. I didn't know who I was, what my purpose was, or what the point of it all could be. Waking up every morning felt like a chore, a never-ending loop of "have to's" instead of "get to's." I couldn't understand how people could find joy in life when it felt like there was more bad than good. I didn't know it then, but I was young, naïve, and lost, trapped inside my own head while life was happening all around me.

Then, in early 2019, my grandma passed away. She was the light of our family, the glue that held us together, the one who always knew how to make everything feel okay. Losing her shattered something in me, and in everyone else, too. Our family began to crumble under the weight of grief. People started arguing, fighting over money and belongings, forgetting the true meaning of family. I couldn't wrap my head around it. How could anyone benefit from her loss? How could they tear each other apart over something so meaningless, when we had just lost the one person who was our peace?
She was my rock, the one who made me feel like I belonged. Losing her made me question everything: life, fairness, and even faith. I didn't understand why someone so pure, so full of love, had to go. And just as I was drowning in that confusion, the

Universe handed me something even heavier.

The Unexpected Diagnosis

It started with an excruciating pain in my lower right abdomen. It was sharp and unrelenting, like someone was twisting something inside of me. But I brushed it off. In my family, I'd always been labeled as "sensitive" or "overly emotional," and I didn't want to be seen as the girl who couldn't handle a stomachache. So, I ignored it.

The pain worsened until I couldn't walk. I was doubled over, sobbing, unable to stand upright. Finally, I told my mom I needed to go to the hospital; I didn't care if I sounded dramatic.
The second I got there, everything happened in a blur. Nurses swarmed around me, prepping me for emergency surgery. It turned out that my appendix was about to burst. I was rushed into the operating room, no time to think, just pain, panic, and bright white lights.

When I woke up, something felt off. I should've felt better, or at least relieved that the surgery went well. But there was a heavy gloom in the air, the same darkness that had followed me since my grandma's passing, only thicker now.

The doctor came in with a look I'll never forget. He said the surgery was successful… but that they had found something unexpected.
A mass. In my bladder.

I didn't understand what that meant. A mass? I was sixteen. That was something you heard adults talk about in whispers, not something that could be happening inside me. I had no idea that moment would split my life in two: the "before" and the "after."

Facing Cancer

Once I healed from the surgery, my world turned into a series of doctors' offices, blood tests, and scans. At sixteen, life was supposed to be carefree… Friday night football games, friends, and dreaming about the future. But mine became about survival. The biopsy results came back. I'll never forget sitting in that cold room, the doctor's lips moving, but everything else going silent. Malignant. Tumor. Cancer.

I was diagnosed with Papillary Urothelial Carcinoma, a rare form of bladder cancer. My doctors were baffled. Only a little over a hundred cases like mine had been recorded since the 1920s. There was no clear path forward, no blueprint for treatment. Just questions, fear, and blank stares.

My mom didn't stop for a second. She became a force of nature, calling every specialist she could find, refusing to take "we don't know" for an answer. I don't think I've ever seen anyone fight like she did.

But even with her strength, I felt helpless.

My life, my body, wasn't mine anymore.
School didn't matter. College didn't matter.
The future didn't matter. I didn't know if I even had one.

Depression hit me harder than ever before. I stopped caring about everything I used to love. My friends drifted away. They said I wasn't "myself" anymore. And they were right. I wasn't.

I didn't recognize the girl staring back at me in the mirror, with hollow eyes, dark circles, and a permanent ache in my chest. My mind was in chaos, like a tornado of fear, confusion, and grief that wouldn't stop spinning.

I was completely lost.

A Miracle and a Message

But through all the darkness, one thing became clear. I remembered my grandma.

I started to believe that maybe she hadn't just left, maybe she was still here, watching over me, guiding me. Maybe she left when she did to save me?
If I hadn't been diagnosed with appendicitis, that tumor would have gone undetected until it was too late. The doctors told me that cases like mine were usually found after symptoms, when it was already terminal. It was a miracle that it had been discovered at all.

And I knew exactly who to thank.

That realization changed me. It was like something inside me woke up. A whisper that said, "You're meant to be here." I started searching for peace within my storm. I turned to spirituality, meditation, and self-care. I practiced yoga daily- not just the poses, but also the connection between breath, body, and spirit. I even began my 200-hour yoga teacher training, diving deep into the mind-body connection.

For the first time, I felt calm. I felt power in stillness. My body might have been fragile, but my spirit was fierce. I started to radiate energy outward, speaking gratitude and positivity into existence… and slowly, the universe responded.

The doctors finally came back with answers. A treatment plan. Hope. And just like that, I was told I was in remission. I was

CANCER FREE.
It felt like the world had colour again.

The Night My Life Changed Forever

But life wasn't done teaching me yet.

It was summer, a few months after remission. I was finally feeling like a normal teenage girl again, hanging out with friends, laughing, breathing freely. When, out of nowhere, I got sick.
At first, I thought it was just a cold. Then it hit harder. I couldn't eat or drink. I started throwing up constantly. My eyes swelled almost completely shut and every blood vessel burst. I looked unrecognizable.

Soon, I was back in the hospital, the place I thought I'd escaped. My oxygen levels kept dropping, my body shutting down. They rushed me to the ICU, hooked me up to machines and flooded my veins with medications I couldn't even pronounce. Still, nothing worked.

And then, one night, everything went black.

I couldn't see, but I could hear. The blaring of alarms. The pounding of footsteps. The chaos of voices shouting. And then, my mom's voice, trembling— whispering in my ear:
"It's okay, honey. You're going to be okay. Don't leave me."
Those were the last words I heard before everything went silent.

And then… peace.

I can't explain it in human words. There was light… a radiant, warm, glowing energy that wrapped around me like a hug. It felt safe, welcoming. Familiar. Like home. I felt weightless.
I felt free.

And in that moment,
I realized I had a choice:
to stay, or to go.

All my life, I had been indifferent to living. Death never scared me; in some strange way, it almost comforted me. From a young age, I often wondered what the point of life was, why people fought so hard to stay when it felt so heavy to exist. I didn't fear dying; I feared living without purpose. Through my journey with cancer, I had started to find glimpses of peace, but I still held onto that quiet detachment, thinking that if my time came, I would accept it.

But in that moment, standing on the edge between this world and whatever comes next, something shifted. That indifference vanished. For the first time in my life, I wanted to live. I wanted to feel the sun on my face again, to laugh, to grow, to love, to experience every single thing this world had to offer.
I chose life.

When I woke up, my mom was right there, tears streaming down her face, holding my hand like she never wanted to let go. Seeing her was the most beautiful thing I could have imagined. That was the moment my outlook on life changed forever.

It was like being given a second heartbeat… a reminder that every breath, every sunrise, every single mundane moment is a gift. That experience shattered everything I thought I knew about life and death. It stripped me of fear, of apathy, and replaced it with something I never expected: gratitude. From that day forward, I wasn't just alive… I was living. And for the first time, I understood what it truly meant to choose life.

Choosing Life

After that night, I knew. There is something beyond this world… something powerful, magical, and full of light. I no longer doubted the energy that connects us all.

I realized that life itself is a miracle. Every sunrise, every breath, every laugh… is a gift. We are given the chance, every single day, to create, to feel, to love, to live.
I used to wake up wondering what the point of life was. Now, I wake up knowing that this is the point… to live, to choose, to grow.

I am grateful for every painful moment… for my cancer, my near-death, and every dark night that brought me here. Because without them, I would have never found the version of myself I am today.

Life will always throw curveballs.
There will always be chaos and uncertainty. But we get to choose how we respond.

We get to choose whether to fall apart or to rise.

So, choose life.

Choose joy.

Choose peace.

Choose to become the best version of yourself, again and again… because every single day, you are given the *gift* to do just that.

Reflection

Writing this story allowed me to relive some of the hardest, darkest moments of my life, but also to honor the incredible light that came from them. For a while, I viewed my past with resentment and pain. During that time, I couldn't understand why life had to happen the way it did, or why I had to experience so much loss and fear at such a young age.

But through time, healing, and reflection, I've realized that those experiences shaped me into who I am today. Resilient, grounded, and at peace with myself. My cancer didn't define me; it awakened me. It taught me that even in the moments where you feel powerless, you still have one of the greatest powers of all… *choice*.

I learned that choosing life isn't just about surviving. It's about waking up every day and deciding to live fully, to embrace the chaos, to love deeply, and to grow endlessly. I'm grateful for the pain, because it showed me the beauty of being alive.

This story isn't just about overcoming illness… It's about transformation, self-discovery, and learning that freedom comes when you finally decide to live as your truest, best self.

Norie Scott

Chapter 9
The Greatest Gift

The Greatest Gift

It was the beginning of 2025.
My boyfriend and I had been getting pretty serious.
We were dating for 3 years now, but I'd known him since we were kids. We had just moved into our first place together, an apartment. Aside from my brother, I had never lived with a boy before. My boyfriend, Dontae, had good morals, and my grandma, Margie, had taught me to pick a man with strong values. Was he organized? Absolutely not. But seriously, he was an overall great guy. One might say he was chosen by God.

We had been living together for a few months when the idea of having children was brought up into the conversation again. "Do you want to have kids?" It had always been a yes ever since I was a little girl. It was the timing I had been waiting for. "Do you want to have kids?" Dontae had been ready since he was in high school, he claimed. At that point, I had been off birth control for a year, so there was a bit of concern.

One evening while sitting alone, I'm not sure exactly what got my mind rolling, but I was very worked up and wept over if I would ever be able to have children. All of a sudden, I dropped down to my knees and asked God to make me fertile. I remember using that exact word. I had my hands together and I was praying. Then the crying stopped and I went on with my night.

Exactly three days later I found out I was pregnant. Wow, wow, wow! I asked God to make me fertile, not pregnant? It seemed as though God's will aligned with mine and my desire to become a mom.
Maybe I knew I was pregnant,
or maybe it just *happened.*

When I took the pregnancy test I said, "I'm not ready." I cried in disbelief, thinking of all the selfish reasons why I didn't want to have a baby, and how I wouldn't be able to pursue my dreams. When in reality, God had placed me *exactly* where he wanted me.

Before that point, I needed a reason to keep living.
I've always been a believer in Christ. My momma and grandma raised me to know God and Jesus. Growing up as a Catholic, I found my love for singing in the church choir.

We all go through times where we fall short of Jesus's feet. I know I did. I found myself back after a horrible accident in college that could have ended in tragedy. By the grace of God, he kept me here. He had *much bigger plans for me.*
One of those strong values I was telling you about, that Dontae had, was Faith.

Dontae had been through his own hell at times, choosing to go down bad roads, to walk away from Christ. Like myself, he always found his way back. *That* was the most appealing detail about Dontae. He knew God. I had never dated anyone who knew God.

One ordinary day, I was headed home from work when Dontae called me, "I'm waiting outside and I can't wait to see you! How was your day?" he said. "It was good, I'm happy," I replied. When I got home, I walked inside and he asked me to sit on the couch. "I have presents for you!" he said. As a lover of presents, and my love language being gifts, I thought "gimme gimme!"

I opened up a baby gift bag, my very first baby present, a little soft soccer ball and a note.

"Read it from the top to bottom," he begged. The note spoke of how happy he was about living with me, that it was his first time living with a woman. We were growing up together, and that was a beautiful thing. He was excited for our baby to arrive, and oh, also,"Will you make me the happiest man alive?" He got down on one knee. He pulled out the most beautiful ring I had ever seen. It was exactly what I told him I wanted a year back in Calabasas, CA.

When we were playing dress up, trying on half a million-dollar rings at the store. I was honestly in shock. I kind of stuttered. "Are you serious?" I said. "Yes", he said. "I do!" I laughed and screamed as he pulled out the red roses and the non-alcoholic rosè, and we celebrated. I knew he must love me, considering my hair was in a bun, I had no make up on, and was wearing a silly sweatshirt. I never imagined it would be like that, but it really showed his heart.

Dontae had been telling me about a church he went to for years. He told me how he was baptized there during his adulthood, and that the Pastor was raw and real. Him and I had tried new churches together, all across Cincinnati. We liked them, but they didn't make us feel at "home". Last Fall we were invited to the church he had been talking about, *Access.*
At the second church service, I was sold. I asked to join the Worship Team that day with no anxiousness. I enjoyed the music and was already learning the lyrics and envisioning myself on stage with the girls and the musicians. I submitted my demo track, and I was in.

As anything does, it takes time for people to get to know you; when you start a new job, new group, new anything. It took some time for most of the girls to get to know me, but when I started my first meeting with the choir, a few of the girls instantly approached me and to greet me and give me hugs. Their smiles seemed real and exciting. I still remember the day I had my pregnancy stick in my black sweatpants on stage before practice. "I have an announcement!" I said. It seemed as if my team leader could read my mind. "Do you want to use the microphone for that Paige?" "I sure do!" I said with a smile. I pulled it out and announced, "I'm pregnant!"

I had no idea what the future 9 months would hold, but everyone was so supportive and happy for me. God put me on that team for support as a woman, and as someone who was going through pregnancy. Every single practice they asked me how I was doing. It was different from the girls at work, or my friends, and I was very grateful.

When I say we were excited for the gender reveal, I can't even properly describe the impatient waiting we were all incurring. I have never seen so many of my family and friends in one place. "Bring diapers for a boy, and wipes if you think it's a girl!" I wrote on the invitation. We were absolutely blessed that day with an enormous stash of both.

I found out I was pregnant in March, and I told my mom about my pregnancy a few months before the gender reveal. On Mother's Day, I gave my mom her present by putting my positive pregnancy test inside her present. Like mother, like daughter, she said the same exact thing: *"I'm not ready."* I confirmed to her I was praying for a baby, and I knew it had happened so soon, but this was a blessing.

She was SO excited for the gender reveal. Her very first grandbaby! If it was a girl, it was to be Lily. If it was a boy, Matteo David. From the very first night I found out I was pregnant, Dontae and I thought it was our little boy. Dontae had that name picked out for his son when he was 16.

There was no argument,
it was going to be Matteo.

The heartbeat had been showing up in the high 150's during the beginning appointments, so that was tricking me some, making me think it might actually be a girl. We had the anatomy scan done and asked to have the gender written on a piece of paper. We gave that paper to my brother Jacob, and his girlfriend Norie. I still have no idea how they didn't spoil the surprise.

Before the big reveal happened, I walked over to a tree at the park, I knew a few people were watching, and I said a prayer. "Please let this be right for our family, for dad and I to not be upset with the answer" I asked. I walked over to the balloon box, Dontae and I put our hands on it, lifted, and…. blue balloons! We knew it! Matteo David was entering this world!

I let my prayer warriors know that day that I wanted them praying for me to have an easy pregnancy. I even believed it for myself. Just as my mom told herself when she had me, an easy pregnancy, labor, and a beautiful special baby was to come. I didn't have much trouble with my pregnancy at all. I know for a fact that prayer changes people's lives.
About halfway through the pregnancy the doctors told me I had a low-lying placenta. They said it could have been the reason I was spotting some, and having some light cramps. They advised me early on if it didn't move up, I wouldn't be able to deliver naturally.

That wasn't my birth plan at all. My goal was to give birth vaginally, with a labor that was induced on its own. Being more holistic, I would prefer to have a natural childbirth, while if necessary, using an epidural for support.

We went in for our 30 week ultrasound, and just like magic, the placenta had moved to the perfect spot and we were back on track again for a natural birth. Matteo's heartbeat was great, and mine was excellent.

I didn't struggle with any health issues or gestational diabetes, I prayed on this, and I ate a well-rounded vegetarian diet throughout my entire pregnancy. I didn't even have any extra aches or pains, other than what was normal.

Once I started my registry online, I started acting like a crazy person. I truly was worried at one point that not a single thing was going to be bought. Fast forward, everything was bought and more. "And my God will meet all your needs according to the riches of his glory in Christ Jesus" Philippians 4:19.

Dontae and I had been looking for a house well before we got that apartment together. I was scared. He was ready to jump, I was not. How? How could we possibly have a house? Sure, I had a great job, and so did Dontae, but I didn't think we were the kind of people that could make it happen. I underestimated myself. But that was okay, I wasn't ready then, and something even better appeared.

Suddenly, one of Dontae's childhood friends, a realtor, convinced us to go see a house. I had a feeling in the pit of my stomach that morning, this might be the one? I said a prayer before we left the apartment, "God, if this is right, tell me". We drove to a neighborhood further away than I imagined living. God told me, it was right. We signed the *same day. My mom was worried because the house was out in the country, further away from family. I told her we already put money down to hold it for us.*

She was shocked. She laid out her concerns of me having a newborn child and no one to rely on during the night while Dontae was working third shift. A few days later she came out and saw it, right before the sun was setting, it was truly a beautiful evening.

"You know my grandma Margie kept saying our cousins were moving to a new development in the same town, that's weird, right?" I told my mom. We laughed, "ok grandma, we get it" I thought. My mom, Dontae, and I were outside looking at the house when I said, "Mom, what if that is our cousins house, really, it's a ranch style home like they said they bought." My mom took a picture and sent it to my cousin. She replied seconds later, "that *is* our house."

My mom started screaming and crying tears with joy, "Oh God is good, he is so good."
Every single miracle that could have happened during my pregnancy, did. Some people may look at me and call me lucky, but I know I've made good decisions and have stayed close to God during this whole 10-month ride.
Yes, pregnancy is not 9 months, they lied to us.

Can you see how God put me at that church right before I became pregnant-to prepare me for this journey with him. The sobriety I was about to endure, the completely different scenery around me, and so much more. As I write this today, I am a month and a half away from my due date, which is December 19, 2025. A Christmas baby we are hoping for! You'll have to follow my socials and reach out to me directly with my email, all in my biography, to stay updated on me and baby "Tao's" life!

Prayer saved my life seven years ago when I was hit by a car as a pedestrian. I was unconscious for several minutes laying in the
100

pouring rain on the concrete. I don't know where I went, or what conversation I had with God, but my life changed forever at that moment. I became a different person, a more well-rounded one. A lot of people prayed for me, and I believe that's one of the reasons my brain didn't turn out worse than it did. I was very fortunate. I reflect on that time often, and realize it's a miracle I can walk, talk, and have children. I am a testimony of living a miraculous life. I have seen many evils in my life, but I have forgiven every single one of them.

If I sat down and told you everything I went through, that Podcast would last hours. But I chose to see the good. I chose to make something better of my life. And you can too.

I prayed every day of my pregnancy. I believe someone else out there prayed for me every day of my pregnancy too. I actually know it, because at least my boyfriend and mom were saying prayers every day! Prayer saves lives. Prayers lift up lives. So, I invite you to pray and worship every day. Are there things missing in your life? Pray and believe 100% they will come true, and they shall.
It does not matter where you've been, or what your past looks like, you deserve a beautiful life too, and I believe in you girls, (and guys)!

Carrying a baby for the first time… the most magical, beautiful, interesting, scary experience of a woman's life. My only hope is that the woman is supported by God, her female friends, spouse, and family. -Paige Nichole Knechtly

*"I prayed for this **child**
and the Lord has granted me what I asked of him."*
1 Samuel 1:27

Thank you to my beautiful mother, inside and out, who let me be a part of this wonderful book, women inspiring women, lives on forever.

Paige Knechtly

Chapter 10

MAKE IT TILL YOU MAKE IT

MAKE IT TILL YOU MAKE IT

I knew my diagnosis was a death sentence when the doctor spoke with tears in his eyes...the stark white of the hospital walls clashed with his light sandy blonde hair. He spoke gently to me, you're far too young to be here.

We don't have many options for you...

"YOU HAVE CANCER my dear, I'm so sorry. I wish there was something else I could say to you."

I stared at him, waiting for him to say something more, but all that was left was the sting of his prickled words.

I walked out the front door gasping for air.

I replayed that moment over and over trying to make sense of what he said to my mind, and then my heart.

I had 2 beautiful kids, and was married to my high school sweetheart. The baby was a senior that year...People always wanted what I had. They didn't know all the sacrifices it took, to make it all look like a story book.

I didn't feel or look sick. That was the oddest feeling, to reconcile the two...

I sat in that lobby waiting for my turn for treatment, it reminded me of herding cattle as they called out names. One out, the next in, next, out...

I don't know why this made me laugh at that thought...little twisted humor I guess at the time...to escape the reality.

About that many people sitting around…trying not to die.

Surrounded by sad hopeless faces, the heaviness in that room week after week...was like being at a funeral with pretentious smiles, you know the ones...you know darn well the deceased didn't like to bring you flowers and shake your hand to be polite.
No one dared to laugh in there...no one truly smiled...

Walking tombstones, is what I saw, a reminder that death was not just all around me.

It was coming for me too...

I had always been a person of deep faith. The WHY's to God became like gravel in my mouth with each prayer I prayed.

I was mad at God and for good reason...cancer and a divorce …REALLY!! God, I would say…as if I should be immune...

A still small voice never left my side when I wailed and threw my fist to the most high.

I had often heard all my life...

Fake it till you make it...but that was crap and I knew it.

I wanted to make it while I make it!!

So I took the hurt and anger and I prayed...Jesus don't let this take root in my heart...sometimes that was all I could say.

I knew where bitterness came from...women scorned for life from a cheating partner and left to die.

I didn't want to be remembered that way.

I couldn't allow what had been done to me rot me from the inside.

I remember the way my mother talked about my father. How she spewed and cursed his name...I wasn't so worried about cancer killing me.

I knew if I allowed this to grow...

I'd dig my own grave...

JESUS!!! Give this pain purpose while you heal my body and my heart...make no mistake I was still mad when I prayed...at times the anger and tears was all I had say.

It was STILL a prayer as I called
HIS name...

I decided to stop...just STOP! I said this twice to reflect on...my mind was the battlefield...I wasn't going to be a slave. I stopped wavering and set my mind on things above.

I WOULD MAKE IT TILL I MAKE IT...

I was no victim or a cattle(insert giggle) I've been a scrapper my whole life, I knew how to rope & ride...I didn't come this far to just lay down & die.

Day 1 of 30 rounds...I woke up with a new plan....how can I make this not about me? Beauty for ashes, strength for fear I set in my heart. I determined I knew my God had more for me than what I could physically see.

Every day for 6 weeks I woke up to praise God anyway...for we don't wrestle against flesh and blood, but against principalities, against powers, against the rulers of the darkness of this world, against spiritual wickedness in high places.

This I knew to be TRUE...

I buried verse Ephesians 6 as a weapon to use...

I made sure I had my joke to tell, humor was my go to...if I could make myself laugh...

Well then I could make you laugh too.

So I fixed my hair, put on my makeup and favorite outfit so I could go to radiation therapy. I was going MAKE IT TILL I MAKE IT!!

Why do you ask, would I even care what I looked like? Well, it's like after being sick for a few days you're finally feeling better and you finally get dressed and hit the town, now you feel more alive and more like yourself, instead wallowing in all of your snotty ole mess.

If I was going to MAKE it till I MAKE IT, I wasn't going to look like what I was going through.

NO cancer was going to take my mascara from me too.

I was determined to take focus off the things that tried to attach themselves to me…

with that...

I focused on storing up my legacy...

That meant letting go…burning everything I had planned down to the ground.

I was going to help others, this wasn't all about me...that I knew other patients, doctors and nurses, could see HOPE isn't lost to anyone who believes.

God of yesterday is still the God of today,

and no grave could hold His name.

I would be no victim...as everything, I mean everything fell apart .

That husband of mine was cheating...as I fought for my life. 20 years together gone...it was my dream to go from a small country home to a big bright house in the suburbs...all the sacrifices I made I would think about.

I was so angry many nights, he drank them away...
Gardening had always been my escape. I loved my flower beds ...it was my sanctuary, it was my safe place...hey made my heart smile...I had dreamed not of a house but for this...

I loved to share them, often the kids on the block would come down to pick from the wildflower garden and make a bouquet for their mom...

A gift and a reminder that having a garden is hoping for tomorrow ..

I'd tear up as they skipped back home, anxiously awaiting to give them away.

The day I moved ...my Daises, my absolute favorite flower...with a broken body and heart, I took that shovel out in the cold March rain...on a mission that I would have this again someday.

But if they died I knew I would never look at a daisy or God or even me the same.

In the spitting rain and sleet, covered in mud…my snot and tears frozen to my face.

Rocky Balboa had nothing on me that day...

I dug each root up as my spirit screamed...NOT FAIR GOD!! To uproot something so beautiful!! With the flutter of your eyelash you can make all this new..

I know how big you are God, I would say. I don't doubt it. This is stupid!! I'm pissed off!! Haven't I suffered enough?

So you're going to take my favorite flowers too...I scoffed...all this going on and I'm worried about flowers I think to myself...I whimpered, as I saw myself for what I had become. A muddy ugly mess driven down to the dirt.

The still, small voice was still there…I tried to ignore Him…it was my way to pay Him back…you've done enough I think so I'm not talking back like a child who doesn't get their way.

You know this is where I used to talk to you Jesus…it will never be the same again (I pout.)

A still, small voice came as tiny whispers carried on around me in the biting wind.

STILL HE SPOKE...

MAKE IT TILL YOU MAKE IT...

I heard again and again...

I left that beautiful house behind and moved for the first time in my life…

alone.

It had a small flower bed, the landlord said...

"I will take it!" I replied. So that 840 sq. ft. apartment became known as the she shed that day.

I always wanted one of those ya know...that ex-husband of mine always said, well...

He didn't do anything, so to me that was just a no.

It's still March, we all know you can't plant anything till May. Cincinnati weather has spring and winter on the same day.

I took my shovel yet again...back into the cold I go...I know my new neighbors thought I had lost my mind ,
I was mad but with FAITH.
I planted those roots with mad faith with each one I sat to say...

I pray for your healing, I pray for your growth, I pray for you to see the sun again, I pray you bloom brighter than you had before. I pray you forgive me for what I didn't know.
I looked out each day and saw they had stayed rooted, strong... they did not bend.
As days went by I never failed to check them, expecting I would look.
One day there it was! As spring came, the bright green of new leaves appeared as signs of NEW life made its way back to me. It was like lightning hitting my heart...I jumped and shouted with excitement when the first one bloomed...

I wept in deep thankfulness when I saw my reflection in them... they had been a representation of my life as they healed and began to bloom.
SO DID I...
I will make something beautiful out of this new life...Daisies are not just for me but for all the world see, good foundation, strong roots is all you need...
TO MAKE IT TILL I MAKE IT...

So this became my mantra as I pressed on..
My whole life I spent for them, no husband, kids now grown...
Was I alone or was I free?
This would be my next journey while navigating the time line of my life the doctors set for me...

Sabrina Morley

Chapter 11

Is the Glass Half Empty or Half Full?

Is the Glass Half Empty or Half Full?

Have you ever felt like something was missing or that you are not totally fulfilled?

I pride myself on always having my life together and in order. My life has been amazing and happy! My story is not uncommon. If any of you have experienced being an empty nester, then you know that feeling of having a void in your life.

Being an empty nester is when the children that you raised, finally move out to start life on their own.

Both of my children moved out within 6 months of each other. I felt like my whole identity was ripped away and I found myself completely at a loss. I had defined myself as the caretaker of the family and now, that was gone. It was a humbling experience to realize that I wasn't needed in that role anymore. If you have gone through this yourself, you know the feeling. It becomes clear when your tasks in life are about to change!

What was I going to do with my time? Perhaps I would go back to work part-time or full-time. Well, you know that old saying, opportunity usually knocks when you least expect it.

Well, it did!

I was talking to a friend, Roberta Campbell, whom I've known for years. She is an author, a podcast host and had taken classes over the course of a year to become a life coach, and transformational teacher.

My friend encouraged me to think about my situation and realize the potential of taking charge of my own destiny. We talked about how to turn my thoughts and attitude into a more positive outlook on the world.

I needed that positivity, and the hope of a better me.

I was learning so much and finally could understand that my future could be whatever I wanted it to be. Along with practicing these principles, I started to learn about manifestation and gratitude. Manifestation is the art of bringing your desires into reality by aligning your thoughts, feelings, and energy with what you want to create.

STARTING THE PROGRAM

There is a saying in our society about the glass half empty or half full. I'm sure you have heard of it. She asked me to think of 50 things that I wanted in my life. It could be anything. Nothing was out of the realm of too big or too elaborate.

She began to have me dream of things that would make me happy. I understood that she wanted me to open my mind and imagine whatever my heart desired. I forgot what that felt like. I had put those dreams and desires on a shelf somewhere in my memories. So, I wrote them down! We then started learning about the way I was raised. This part was very important because it shaped me from an early age to see the world in a positive or negative light. Until Roberta discussed this, I had never even thought about my outward attitude and how it could be detrimental to success in my life! I had been brought up in a home that spoke negative attitudes constantly. This is called our reprogramming. I learned how to change those thoughts and words into a positive spin on everything in my life.

The program and training allowed me to change the way I thought about all aspects of my life. The term for this is called the Law of Vibration. It is the idea that our thoughts and emotions are all considered energy in motion. By aligning your thoughts and vibration, you start to attract those things you truly desire into your life.

Another law that compliments this idea is the Law of Attraction. By aligning your vibration, you attract positive experiences into your life through positive thoughts, helping you move toward your goals. In contrast, negative thoughts and words can hold you back from reaching your true potential.
A huge part of this is to be grateful and thankful for all things in your life, situations and daily living!

By changing the paradigm of the old habits of negativity in your life into the positive ones, you can change your future into anything you want. By being grateful, I was able to consciously change my attitude and the way I viewed the world into a positive, loving point of view. I started to respond to situations instead of harshly reacting to them. I now see how being thankful and grateful can humble you and allow you to see the bigger picture of purpose in this life.

TRANSFORMATIONS

When I started this program, I was searching for a way to better myself and learn how to manifest my dreams into my life. It has become so much more than that. At first, I learned about myself. I thought about that statement and exclaimed "I know who I am!" But, did I really love everything about me or my personality? The truth was that I didn't like many things about my personality or confidence anymore. I had become bitter and super negative about situations and people. I had to take a hard look inward and ask "Who am I now since my children have left? Do I like what I am seeing in myself?"

I began to take an evaluation of my life and realized that I needed to change my ways of negativity and judgement of others. I believe the hardest part of self-evaluation is to acknowledge the bad flaws and the ugliness of your heart!
116

I didn't want to be tainted with all these negative qualities of my thought process anymore! I found the hardest critic of me was myself. Why did I have all of this negative self-talk, attitude towards things in my life?

Well, I learned that it was the subconscious programming of our upbringing when we were little children. But for me, it had become a nasty crutch that had begun to grow over the years like a disease. I learned that I had to change my perception—and the attitude I was portraying. How do you do that? By becoming aware of what comes out of your mouth and by policing those limiting, negative thoughts! It's called awareness of your words and thoughts and turning those negative words into something more positive!

I'll give you an example of one. Every time I was given a compliment, I would turn it into something negative. " You look really pretty with your hair like that." My reply was "I hate my hair, it never does what I want it to do!" Instead of saying thank you, I would always deflect that comment into something bad! Changing your awareness of what comes from within, is a great start to changing your negative patterns.

I started to learn that I needed to love myself first before I could project that image of positivity outward. So, I began putting in the work. I started using positive affirmations and becoming more aware of my words and thoughts. I wanted to attract that positive vibe back into my life. So, I began to alter my thinking and I became a confident, healthy, positive woman! I wanted to be my authentic self and for others to love me for who I was becoming.

Along with trusting in the process of the program, God and myself, I was noticing change and calmness. A huge part of change has come from being thankful and grateful for all I have, and for the things that will come in the future. When we truly believe things will happen in our lives because we've asked for them, then why not be thankful for future blessings now?

Always have an abundance of gratitude and thankfulness in your life. In the bible, there is a verse that states "Ask and it will be given to you; seek and you will find; knock and the door will be opened to you." Matthew 7:7.

I adopted this mentality for my life and I have a lot less anxiety and worry about the future. Imagine things and situations going the way you want them to. Please do not worry about things you cannot control. Let God do the controlling!

LAW OF RHYTHM

By embracing daily struggles, I learned that this program can be applied to every aspect of my life. I learned to trust more, love stronger, heal from the trauma of my past and have less anxiety. During the process of learning from the course, Roberta challenged me to read a book called, *A Return to Love* by Marianne Williamson.

In the book, the author talks about how life can be up one minute and down the next. Situations can turn bad in an instant and turn wonderful the next day. These ups and downs are part of our life journey. She states "What we can change, however, is how we perceive them. And that shift in our perception is a miracle."

This concept of ebb and flow is known as the Law of Rhythm. It teaches that life moves cycles, seasons and patterns. Our lives are part of this natural rhythm. We are all on different journeys, each with its own highs and lows.

As I examined the program, I began to find many similarities with the way I was raised. My parents were strict but very loving. We were raised going to church our entire childhood into adulthood. My guidelines for this program mirrored many aspects of faith and love that I already knew and trusted. Whether you believe in God or a higher power in the universe, or whatever your belief system, the principles are very similar. God is love! Leading with love in all aspects of your life can be the most rewarded way to live.

Just like the Law of Rhythm stated, I would soon find myself in that up and down flow. I went back to work part time but did not love the job I was doing. I kept telling myself that I was grateful for having a job. However, I looked for the positive in all things, even my job I didn't prefer at the time. One day, my husband came to me and told me he had been laid off. I was shocked, but happy. Yes, happy, because he hadn't liked the job or employees he worked with. He'd been miserable. I held on to the belief that he would find a better job, one he truly loved.

I believed that by being positive and grateful, he would find something much better. He is still searching for a good fit and I have faith that he will find it. I am already grateful for the job he will find in the future. Everything always works out. Fortunately, I had a job land in my lap. One with great benefits and better pay. A job that I enjoy. And I am so very thankful!

Another situation that has happened to me was my father's slow decline with Alzheimer's. In January, it will be 6 years living with this disease. In recent months I have seen a sharper decline in his health and memory. My attitude remains strong and positive. My outlook is hopeful, because I know that every day he is still with us is a precious gift.

Sure, I could have taken a pessimistic view of the entire diagnosis. But what would that accomplish? I'm simply grateful to have him here for as long as we can, and any other attitude feels unacceptable. Alzheimer's is hard on the family. It is difficult to watch someone you love decline the way this disease destroys them. With each day, I'm saying a long goodbye and I am grateful for the time we have left. Many people's loved ones are here today and gone tomorrow. I know our days are numbered but having a positive perception makes all the difference!!

I have grown and evolved so much after being in this program. I see things in a new light and I continue to grow everyday. All of the relationships in my life have flourished and become stronger. I have become a better communicator and positive influence on people. This evolution is possible for anyone who desires to have a positive change and learn how to manifest your dreams. It's possible for anyone! You just have to want it!!

Quotes for thought:

- Everything always works out. Tell yourself this and believe it
- Whatever you believe to be true; will be your truth! Understand the power of positivity.
- Nothing is good or bad; only the meaning you give it.

Melina Patrick

The Power of Our Stories

As we come to the close of this anthology, I invite you to pause, take a deep breath, and truly feel the extent of what you've just experienced. Within these pages, you've read the raw, authentic, and courageous stories of women who have faced heartbreak, trauma, and unimaginable challenges. Women who once questioned their worth, their strength, and their future — and yet, they chose to rise.
Every story you've read represents so much more than words on a page.

They are testimonies of transformation, proof that healing is possible, and reminders that no matter where you've been, your past does not define you.
These women didn't just share their experiences. They opened their hearts, peeled back layers of pain, and allowed you to witness their journeys of becoming whole again. They chose to heal from the inside out— to release what no longer served them, to embrace forgiveness, and to step boldly into their chosen new identities. And here's the truth, you can too.

The Ripple Effect of Healing

One of the most beautiful things about sharing our stories is the ripple effect it creates. When one woman heals, she doesn't just heal herself— she creates space for her family, her friends, and her community to heal as well.

Her courage becomes a light for others still lost in the dark, a whisper of hope for someone wondering if change is possible. Each chapter in this book represents a light being turned on in the world. And together, these lights form a brilliant star, guiding the way for others to follow.

Your Journey Starts Now

As you close this book, I want you to remember something:
The power you've read about here does not only exist in these authors. It lives inside of you, too.

Maybe you saw yourself in one of these stories.
Maybe you felt a stirring in your soul as you read about the breakthroughs and triumphs these women experienced.

That stirring is your intuition whispering, "It's time."
It's time to let go of the weight you've been carrying.
It's time to forgive yourself for the past.
It's time to unleash the woman you were always meant to be.

An Invitation to Rise

When I first envisioned *UnleashHer*, I dreamed of creating a safe, sacred space where women could come together to share their truth and find their voice.
What began as an idea has now blossomed into a sisterhood —
a tribe of strong, authentic women lifting each other higher.

This anthology is just the beginning.
If these stories have touched your heart, let them be a catalyst for your own journey.

You don't have to do it alone.
Join us. Step into a community of women who are committed to healing, growth, and living fully aligned, authentic lives.
Because when you rise, we all rise.

Conclusion: Your Becoming Begins Here

As you close this book, carry with you the truth seen in every woman's story: healing begins within, and transformation is possible for anyone who is willing to rise. These women did not just survive their experiences — they reclaimed themselves, reawakened their power, and stepped into lives filled with clarity, courage, and joy.

My hope is that their words remind you of your own strength...your own voice…your own readiness to become the woman you were always meant to be.

Your journey doesn't end here.
In many ways, this is where it truly begins.

If you feel called to continue awakening, healing, and living from a place of joy, freedom, and authenticity, I invite you to stay connected with me. Visit my website for inspiration, tools, and guidance designed to help you **UnleashHer**— the powerful, intuitive, extraordinary woman within you.

Thank you for being part of this sisterhood, this movement, and this unfolding.
May you continue to choose yourself, honor your journey, and discover the joy of truly living.

Your next chapter is calling.
And it's yours to write.

Roberta Campbell

About the Authors

The Fall and Rise of Roberta Campbell

Roberta Campbell is a highly driven woman with a natural gift for helping others transform their lives. Transitioning from a hairstylist to entrepreneur, Roberta is a 3x author, a keynote and motivational speaker, a publisher, a transformational teacher, mentor and podcast host for *UnleashHer* podcast. As an entrepreneur, Roberta is on a mission to EMPOWER Women to Embrace Their Authenticity and Create an Extraordinary Life.

https://www.robertacampbellofficial.com/
Robertacampbellofficial@gmail
Facebook- Roberta Campbell
Intsagram-Robertacampbellofficial
YouTube-Robertacampbellofficial
LinkedIn-Roberta Campbell

Success is a Sure thing for You

Chantelle Sprenger is an Elevation Coach, author, and founder of the SMILES™ Method. A transformational framework that empowers both children and the adults who guide them. Her work fuses neuroscience, energy awareness, and mindset practice to help families, educators, and children grow in confidence, calm, and clarity. What began as a passion for empowering kids expanded after her own burnout, evolving into a movement rooted in self-regulation, imagination, and identity elevation. Through her courses, books, and coaching, Chantelle is redefining how we raise and educate the next generation, because when one adult rises, a child's world expands. Elevating the future, one SMILE at a time.

Smilesempowerkids@gmail.com
https://bio.link/empoweredgeneration
TikTok: @chantellesprenger
Instagram: smilesempower

The Girl in the Mirror

Stephanie Harrell is a certified relationship and life coach, motivational speaker, and author dedicated to empowering women to reclaim their voice, their power, and their purpose.

Through her own healing journey, she discovered the transformative power of storytelling, visualization, and manifestation— and now helps women rise, heal, and create lives filled with abundance and confidence.

Stephanie is the creator and owner of a powerful framework that guides women through healing, self-discovery, and intentional growth. She is currently expanding her impact as an author and speaker, sharing her message of empowerment and emotional freedom with audiences everywhere. As part of her continued mission to help women build fulfilling, purpose-driven relationships, Stephanie is developing a companion journal for her relationship course, designed to help participants apply the principles in their daily lives.

Facebook: Stephanie Harrell
Instagram: @purposeful.mindset
TikTok: @purposeful_mindset
Email: purposefulmindset1@gmail.com

The Long Road Home

Chantelle Miller is a mirror for truth and light, a bridge for transformation. Through her voice, her breath, and her frequency, she activates codes of remembrance within others. Awakening their ascension and guiding them back to their true essence. Having walked through the depths of darkness, Chantelle now stands as a radiant pillar of light for others, illuminating the path towards healing, expansion, authenticity, and embodied power. As a transformational guide, public speaker, trauma-informed breath-work practitioner and mindset coach, she provides a safe space to hold deeply immersive transformational retreats, she weaves nature, breath, somatics, energy and wisdom to support others in remembering who they truly are to rise into their limitless potential.

www.chantellemiller-mindbodysoul.com
@chantellemillerr - Instagram
Chantelle Miller - Facebook

Visual Frequency Medicine

Jade Breanne Olszewski is an international Christ-centered artist, published author, and founder of the Jade Breanne Collective—a sanctuary for spirit-led art, community, and creative healing. Her work, known as Visual Frequency Medicine, weaves together prayer, intention, and the presence of the Holy Spirit to create paintings that stir the soul and elevate sacred spaces.
After decades of chronic illness, abuse, and losing the use of her dominant arm, Jade experienced a miraculous reawakening that restored her health, faith, and purpose.

Since then, her gold-accented paintings—symbols of divine refinement—have reached collectors across six countries. Her debut book, The Power of Colour, explores the spiritual and emotional impact of colour and how to create peace-filled spaces through faith-rooted design.
Jade's creations are more than art—they're visual prayers for visionary women craving peace, beauty, and sacred reminders of who they truly are.

Website: www.jadebreannecollective.com

IG: @jade.breanne.art
FB: @jade.breanne.art
TikTok: @jade.breanne.art
YouTube: @jade.b.olszewski
Email: hello@jadebreannecollective.com

My Testimony- My Victory

Margaret Tapogna Gatzonis is a spiritual coach, somatic movement guide, and Reiki Master dedicated to helping others awaken to healing, freedom, and joy. Through her signature blend of energy work, mindful movement, and heart-centered mentorship, she empowers individuals to restore balance and reconnect with their inner light. Recognizing each person as a whole being—body, mind, emotions, and spirit—Margaret guides transformation from the inside out. Her mission is rooted in divine love and the belief that true healing begins when spirit and movement unite: Affirming her mantra "When spirit meets movement, love leads the way."

https://www.instagram.com/missmdivinecoaching/?next=%2F
https://www.facebook.com/missmdivinecoaching
https://www.missmdivinecoaching.com

When the Body Screams What the Heart Can't Say

Ashley Marie Crawford is passionate about helping others heal and live as the healthiest, most authentic versions of themselves. Guided by her own journey toward balance and self-discovery, she is currently focused on cultivating a peaceful state of mind while exploring holistic wellness and fitness coaching.

Ashley is also stepping into her next chapter as an author and motivational speaker, inspiring others to embrace healing, growth, and wholehearted living.

TikTok: @enchantress_77785
Instagram: @ashleydmc3
Facebook: Ashley Marie

Choosing Life

Norie Scott is a nursing student and a first-time author whose experience in overcoming serious health challenges ignited her passion for helping others. She is pursuing a career in the medical field to bring healing and hope to those who need it most. Family plays an essential role in Norie's life, grounding her through every chapter of her journey, and inspiring her to live with gratitude and love. She finds joy in yoga, travel, mindful living, and creating in the kitchen through baking and cooking— always embracing life as the beautiful gift that it is.

FB-Emma Scott (Norie)

The Greatest Gift

Paige Knechtly is a strong force to be reckoned with. While she has both sweet and spicy sides, she always stays authentically true to herself. She inspires people through her music; two time album produced records, a best-selling author of the book *She Looks Fine*, and has a following base of over 40k followers.

Paige uses her degree in Public Health to create awareness of healthy living to all. As a soon-to-be mother of one, a fiance, and a woman, Paige inspires all to live their best lives by keeping faith and positivity at the center of their heart.

IG-iampaigeofficial
Youtube-IAMPAIGEOFFICIAL
TikTok-iampaigeofficial_
Paige.knechtly@gmail.com

Make It Till You Make It

Sabrina Morley is a seven-year brain tumour survivor whose journey has become a beacon of hope and resilience. She shares her powerful story with local hospitals and charities, inspiring others to embrace healing, faith, courage, adaptability, and hope. Through her advocacy and compassion, Sabrina reminds others that even in life's darkest moments, light and purpose can emerge. Now stepping into her next chapter as an author, she continues to give back by turning her pain into purpose and her story into inspiration.

FB-Sabrina Morley
IG-Sabrina.Morley
Sabrinablank46gmail.com

Is the Glass Half Empty or Half Full?

Melina Patrick is a positive influencer and visionary who believes in the power of gratitude, faith, and self-growth. A devoted wife and proud mother of two grown children, she continues to evolve and inspire those around her through her unwavering positivity and faith in God's plan.

With the love and support of her husband, Melina is on a journey of continual transformation—learning, growing, and shining her light so others may find their own. Guided by thankfulness and divine purpose, she is creating an extraordinary life filled with love, joy, and limitless potential.

FB: Melina Patrick
Email: Me@melinajp.com

REFERENCES

Williamson, Marianne (1992) A Return to Love Reflections on the Principles of A Course In Miracles. HarperCollins Publishers. Page 17

"I prayed for this child
and the Lord has granted me what I asked of him".
(1 Samuel 1:27)

"And my God will meet all your needs according to the riches of his glory in Christ Jesus" (Philippians 4:19)

"Ask and it will be given to you; seek and you will find; knock and the door will be opened to you." (Matthew 7:7)